SHORTS FROM KENT

Edited by

SUZI BLAIR

NEW FICTION

First published in 1993 by
NEW FICTION
4 Hythegate, Werrington
Peterborough,
PE4 7ZP

Printed in Great Britain by Forward Press.

Copyright Contributors 1993

This book is sold subject to the condition that it shall not,
by way of trade or otherwise, be lent, re-sold, hired out
or otherwise circulated without the publisher's prior consent
in any form of binding or cover other than that in which
it is published and without a similar condition including this
condition being imposed on the subsequent purchaser

Foreword

The advent of New Fiction signifies the expansion of what has traditionally been, a limited platform for writers of short stories. New Fiction aims to promote new short stories to the widest possible audience.

The *Shorts* collections represent the wealth of new talent in writing, and provide enjoyable, interesting and readable stories appealing to a diversity of tastes.

Intriguing and entertaining; from sharp character sketches to 'slice of life' situations, the stories have been selected because each one is *a good read*.

This collection of short stories is from the pens of the people of Kent. They are new stories, sweeping across the spectrums of style and subject to reflect the richness of character intrinsic to the region, today.

Suzi Blair
Editor.

Contents

The Compelling Gaze	Jack Clifton	1
Beyond the Sky	James Miller	4
One Lonely Dark Night in a Sussex Cottage	John Baggott	7
Blossom Time	John Allen	10
Burning Ambition	Piers Manser	14
The Twilight Rebel	Pauline Till	17
Amateurs	R J Edwards	21
The Debating Ordeal	Ella Mayes	25
Idle Curiosity	David Topham	29
The Journey	Maureen Cox	33
Injured Parties	Gloria Smith	36
Child's Play	Pam Brown	39
No Time to Explain	Sue Edwards	41
Birds of Paradise	Karen Martyn	43
The Birthday	Anne Hoad	46
Driven	Neil Davies	50
Billy's Dog	Tom Thompson	52
Fatal Attraction	Elisabeth K Cook	56
Administrative Error	John Mattocks	58
Dreaming	Susan Prescott	62
Turkey and Biceps	Tom Buckland	65
Oceans of Guilt	C R A Pennington	69
The Wild Goose Chase	Neville Taylor	73
Rings of Gold	Tessa Lawton	77
Famous Folk From Bristol	Michael Rose	80
The Retreat	Joan Mitchell	83
The Story of How Hannah Lost Her Blues	Gavin Wright	86
King Corn	Michael J Hills	88
Haesten's People	Paul Swaffer	89
A Handsome Stranger	Mavis Foreman	91
Compulsions	Sean R Carter	94
The Shelves Lay Bare	Eileen Ramm	97
Neither Power Nor Glory	Reginald Hunter	102

High Price for a High Rise	Gaye Giuntini	106
The Brandenburger's Bones	Andrew Bowers	108
The Dark Red Rose	Yoni	111
A Talent for Deception	Robert Fish	115
A Time Share Break	C D Doran	119
Forced to Run	Richard Nairn	123
Both Sides of the Coin	Edith Wynne-Williams	125
Going for Gold	Michael Smith	127
Death by Dust	Avril Barwick	130
The Problem Patch	F C Trotter	133
Dying for a Leak	Nigel Hemingford-Grey	135
The Apple Orchard	Tony Bridge	139
Revenge	K L Baseden	143
The Ride to Alice	Julie Lynn	145
The Eagle Has Landed	Stephen Passey	149
Emptiness	Roger Davis	152
In the Beginning	A H Addis	154
The Washing Up	Helen Fairfield	156
A Fare Terminated	Caroline Sumnall	158
To Catch the Wind	Jeni Waterfield	162
A Coat of Many Colours	Simon Taylor	165
Ethel's 'Opping	Nora Veysey	168

The Compelling Gaze

by

Jack Clifton

Paul Clifford was a young man, who even when a small child, had very sensitive feelings. He always felt intensely every emotion that occurred. When growing up, in fact, he took things too seriously and believed there was only one way to life and that was to stick rigidly to correct behaviour.

This conviction towards behaviour influenced him as he grew up and was often the cause of arguments, between him and his many friends. Their way of life was too free and easy for Paul and he despaired sometimes, about how his friends behaved and laughed at conventions.

This narrow attitude was to bring about a very bitter state of mind in him, regarding his girlfriend, Elaine. She was a very fun loving girl, who was a trifle more unconventional than Paul would have liked her to be.

Elaine had many admirers and at dances, was always in great demand, by other young men. She enjoyed the happy atmosphere of the round of dances, tennis and cocktail parties, and was genuinely fond of Paul, but did not realize how seriously he took what he believed should be her behaviour, after they had become engaged.

One evening, a very keen admirer named John Werren had taken every opportunity to dance with Elaine and let her see he was interested in her. This made Paul annoyed and he became very angry and jealous, and rather upset Elaine when he said she was encouraging this man and should rebuff his attentions. This caused Elaine to get angry and she said that there was no harm in stringing this fellow along, as there was no reason why she should shut herself away from other men. Paul could not see it this way and after a row he left her.

After a few drinks in the bar he came back to the dance floor and as Elaine and this John Werren came off the floor he lost his temper and punched this chap on the jaw. He said to Elaine, 'That's the end of our engagement' and walked out of the dance room.

He got into his car and drove away feeling very mad and upset. After a long time driving at speed he slowed down and presently came to an old world hotel in a country area.

Some unknown reason made him stop and he looked at this old building which must have been a country house before being turned into a hotel. Some impulse made him decide to stop the night and he drew up in front of the Hotel door.

When he was booking in he asked the manager if there was any way for him to fix him up with pyjamas and a razor and was assured that this could be arranged. After he had gone to the bar he sat down and had a few drinks with bitter thoughts of what had occurred. He ordered a meal but found he could not manage to eat it.

When he went to bed he lay on his back and with the light still on, he continued to review the evening's happenings. Some impulse made him look at a large painting on the wall at the foot of the bed. It was a painting of a young and pretty girl dressed in old world clothes and as he looked, her eyes seemed to hold his eyes in a positive gaze. The more he tried to ignore her eyes the more he seemed to be drawn back to stare and feel that in her intense gaze she was trying to communicate with him.

He must have dropped off to sleep and in a dream, he saw himself dressed in clothes of an early period sitting in a room in front of a log fire. Just then, a young and beautiful girl came into the room dressed in Elizabethan style clothes. He rose to his feet and greeted her with a fond embrace. She danced away from him and with a roguish smile said, 'I have been asked to spend a few weeks with Lady Jackson and her son Clarence.'

This made Paul very angry and he said, 'I do not want you to go, particularly as Lady Jackson was eager to get her son married to you.'

She laughed and replied, 'But why can't I go, it's a wonderful house they have, with lovely gardens and such grand dinners and dances.'

John became more angry and he told her he did not want her to go, especially as they had not asked him to visit them. She did not realize how mad he was and tossed her head and said, 'I will not be told what to do.'

Paul said, 'You cannot love me when you go against my wishes,' and left the room in a temper saying their engagement was over.

More out of pique, she decided to go and when she arrived at the Jacksons palatial home with her mother they were given a great welcome.

When Paul heard she had gone he became more angry and decided to go with his friends to foreign parts. Her mother and Lady Jackson used all their influence on her to marry Clarence Jackson and when Paul had not sent any message to say he regretted his outburst, and was told that he had left the Country, in a weak moment she was persuaded to marry Clarence.

This marriage was a failure, as she found that Clarence was subject to strange fits and cruel behaviour which made her life so unhappy, also being shut up in a dreary environment.

She got into the habit of going for long walks in the park and one day she was caught in a storm. By the time she arrived back she was wet through. She became very ill, lost her will to live and died.

Paul awoke with a start sweating profusely, and it seemed that the girl in the picture was imploring him not to destroy his life with Elaine as she had done long ago.

This dream had a great effect on Paul and he said to himself, 'What a fool I was to take things too seriously.' As soon as he had bathed, shaved and without breakfast paid his account at the hotel, he jumped into his car and hurried back to see Elaine.

When he saw her at her home he told her how silly he was to get so angry and to throw away her love. He said he loved her and regretted the whole affair and would she forgive him? Elaine was so happy to hear him say this and said she was to blame as well, and she had no intention of any serious feelings for John Werren.

After they were married, Paul told her about the strange story of the girl in the picture. Elaine was intrigued when Paul had told her all the details and she said she would like to visit this hotel and see the picture.

They called one day to the hotel and when they saw the Manager they asked if they could see the room Paul had slept in. When they stood at the foot of the bed and looked at the face of the girl in the picture it seemed to them that she smiled and her eyes twinkled, and as the sunlight flitted over her face she radiated contentment and happiness. As they stole silently out of the room her eyes followed them with a gaze of quiet peace.

Beyond the Sky

by

James Miller

It is strange; I don't even know why I'm bothering to write this. After all, nobody will ever read it. I think I write for the sake of my sanity. I have to find some way of putting these things which are happening to me into some sort of perspective. If I just sat and watched, I would undoubtedly go mad.

I never thought that it would end like this; in fact I never thought I'd see the end. Unless... unless I have died, and all men see this when they die. But... no that is ridiculous. When could I have died? I'm not old enough to pass away in my sleep, not by a long way, and I don't recall doing anything which could lead to my loss of life. Or perhaps that event has been wiped from my memory. Certainly I wouldn't relish the thought of remembering what dying was like. But my writing, like my thoughts drift, fleeing away from the subject in hand.

I'm not yet ready, in fact I can't begin to describe what the end is like. Maybe later... I don't know. Somehow I always thought of Armageddon, if that is an appropriate word, or maybe Judgement Day, as being a vivid, explosive affair. I definitely thought that when, or if, that day ever dawned, I'd realise that it was just that. There would be no space for idle musing or philosophical speculation. I suppose that I never thought the end would be so beautiful.

I was sitting in a garden watching as the last shades of sunlight faded away over the tree tops, so I saw all of the colours in the sky. I remember a vivid white flash which spread across the heavens like a ripple in a pond, losing its brightness and darkening to yellow, then orange then ochre. However, this display of light failed to illuminate the ground below, which remained lost in darkness.

I was not frightened by the lights. There was something calming, soothing really about the display. Watching it, the display seemed to last a few seconds, when in reality I discovered afterwards that it had lasted several hours. It left me feeling disorientated and confused, as if I had been plucked from a deep sleep.

After the display, I went to bed (it was from a clock in the bedroom that I discovered how much time had passed). Everything around me seemed intangible, unreal. It was like walking in a dream, as if I was a passive observer watching myself with no more interest than one watches people on the street strolling past. As I wrapped the duvet around me and turned out the light my thoughts wandered. They turned to dreams and I dreamed a dream which I hadn't had since I was a little child. I dreamed of being sky.

I have not left my house since then. In the morning the sun rose slowly and sluggishly. It hardly seemed to have enough strength to make the effort to turn morning into afternoon. I watched the sun and I watched the things in the sky. By evening, thirty hours later, the sky was laced with a sinewy pattern of delicate traceries. I was reminded of spider webs. And in the woods opposite my house I saw... things. I cannot bring myself to write about them yet.

My sense of dislocation from my surroundings grew as the evening progressed. I would get up from my chair by the window to go and get something to drink, and still feel as though I was sitting down, looking out.

The second night lasted, by the clocks in this house, thirty-six hours. I believe I slept right through. Coming down in the dim light of the early morning I saw the living room with its hard dusty floor boards and mottled faded furniture and thought, this isn't my house. Something of a memory touched me... but in an instant it was gone.

The weird spider webs had covered much of the sky now, distorting its colour and the light which shone through it. It was like looking through a time warped window which had been badly cracked. For a final surrealistic touch I watched as clouds scuttled past underneath the splintering sky, undistorted by the bizarre traceries.

Another night has passed and before bed, I saw those things in the woods again. I feel like they've surrounded the house. I'm very isolated out here, nothing but thick, mystical forest surrounds the house. I slept fitfully that night, perturbed by strange noises in the garden. Somehow I know that this isn't my bed.

The sun hardly managed to rise at all this morning. Twelve hours have passed and it still hovers just above the tree tops. Due to the sky distorting spider webs the sun no longer looks round; in fact it's devoid of shape, is little more than a jumble of light. At least it doesn't hang underneath the sky, like the clouds. That would be too much to cope with.

It is very difficult to write. I keep forgetting what I'm writing about or what the last line said. Sometimes I sit for hours staring into space, gradually becoming aware of what the pen in my hand is for, and what I'm doing. It's early afternoon now, and I can see them gathering in strength in the woods.

Sometimes, like now, I have lucid moments. For an instant I remembered it all; who I am, where I am, what this house is, how I got here. But even as I write the memory starts fading. What remains...? Youth, I was young, a child. Playing games in the woods perhaps? This isn't my house. I really should leave.

Now the woods are full of them; they cluster around the tree trunks and cling to the branches like black sticky tar. I think that they are waiting for something. I daren't go outside. Meanwhile, I can see dark smudges behind blue shards of sky. I think that there is something, waiting behind the sky now. Is it from space?

God. Am I watching God? Now I get up and start to walk somewhere only to stop and stand confused, trying to work out what I'm doing standing up. Sometimes I stand for hours like this.

I think I can remember it all; I did not die, and this isn't purgatory. I don't think it is Judgement day either. I remember saying goodbye to my mother and going off from our house and running into the woods. I remember my mother's hands, they felt so smooth, and the flowers on her dress. I remember little else. The woods! How vividly and vibrantly I feel them. Running now, faster and faster, leaping over logs and ducking underneath branches. Running my hands over the trees and rolling about in the grass. I remember the cool, shadowy light and the way it was broken up into individual golden shafts by the leaves and the twigs. I spoke with my imaginary friends, the people of the forest. I challenged them to come out and show themselves. They were the friends of my childhood. I look out of the window and I don't think that they are so imaginary now.

The shadows in the forest lengthened and darkened, and I had to hurry home. I had never been as deep into the forest as this before, and was lost. After an age of wandering this way and that I discovered a path which led to a tall, old house. It's silhouette is vividly imprinted on my brain as it stood, brooding and menacing against the twilight sky.

I knocked on the door and tapped on the windows in the hope of finding somebody to ask for directions but the house was deserted. Round the back was a large conservatory, connected to the main building. I found a chair and dragged it outside. The sky was clear and I knew that there was going to be an especially beautiful sunset tonight. I planned to watch the setting sun then spend the night in the empty house.

I watched as the sun began to fade from the horizon and the cool of evening came gently down from the stars. I waited for night and my thoughts wandered.

When my time comes, I worried, to be sky; will I fly or will I fall?

One Lonely Dark Night in a Sussex Cottage

by

John Baggott

Lilac cottage occupied a quiet rural position on the edge of a charming West Sussex village. That was how the Estate Agents described it. What they did not point out was that it was opposite a disused cemetery. However it did not worry James, he bought it anyway, love at first sight he claimed, and he had lived there happily for over two years.

He now lay sleeping, his bedroom under the eaves of the seventeenth century cottage he called home. Some thought it isolated, situated as it was at the end of a quiet county lane about half a mile from the nearest neighbour, but being a country lover the relative seclusion suited him. As with all old cottages it had its own familiar noises, but to him the creaks and groans were all part of the character of the place. It was a clear Autumn evening, with not a trace of wind and he had retired early having played a rather energetic squash match after work.

At first he did not hear the noise; he always joked that it would take a bomb to rouse him before the alarm went off, but eventually his brain attuned to whatever it was and he lay wide awake. A quick glance at the clock revealed that it was just after three-thirty. There it was again a sort of howl, a deep yet piercing sound certainly not one he was used to hearing. He now sat up in bed in an effort to concentrate, where was it coming from?

Slowly he slid out of the bed and crept toward the leaded light window. As usual the curtains were not drawn, he preferred it that way. Peering into the darkness he could see very little, but a break in the cloud allowed him to establish there was nothing in the small back garden or the field beyond. Was it a dream, a nightmare perhaps? No, there it was again louder and somehow more menacing now! What should he do? He always told his friends that he was not frightened living, as they put it, in the middle of nowhere: all of a sudden he was not so sure.

Instinct told him to reach for the phone, his hand went for the receiver as if drawn by a magnet, but who he was going to call, he had no idea. He need not have bothered, instead of the reassuring drone of the dialling tone there was nothing, just an eerie silence occasionally interrupted by a quiet crackle. What was happening? His pulse rate quickened, this was stupid. There must be a perfectly logical explanation for all of this. Here he was a grown man of twenty-seven getting himself worked up over nothing.

But why wasn't the phone working? Perhaps he had forgotten to pay the bill, no he distinctly remembered taking it to the Post Office last week. There must be a fault on the line, he would ring them from the office tomorrow and report it. His thoughts were jolted back to the present as the strange sound emitted once more. This time he rushed to the bathroom window at the front of the cottage, again the moonlight provided some illumination but there was nothing to be seen.

Just as he was about to come away from the window James saw a slight movement out of the corner of his eye. There it was again, some sort of shape beside the front gate. Was it the moonlight casting a shadow and playing tricks with his eyes? Until now the room had been in darkness, he reached for the light switch, then thought better of it. If there was something out there, best keep a low profile. With that he crept across the landing back into the bedroom and sat on the old rocking chair and tried to fathom what to do next.

All of a sudden he noticed that the room had somehow become more gloomy, if that was possible! The moon must have disappeared behind the clouds once more. Glancing at the digital clock radio to check how much time had elapsed he noticed the lack of the familiar and somehow reassuring glow of the figures. A frantic rush to the light switch confirmed his worst fears: there was no electricity. Again he reached for the 'phone: nothing. James was now filled with a feeling of complete isolation!

In a blind panic he rushed from one window to another, but even the moonlight had failed him now as he stared into the pitch black night. Somehow the clouds appeared to have stopped moving, everything was totally still. It was a bad dream, it must be, damned realistic but just a bad dream. At that moment he tumbled over the old weight that was used as a door stop. The fall and the resultant blood pouring from a deep gash in his knee convinced him this was reality. You didn't have genuine warm congealing blood even in the most true to life nightmare!

Pulse racing and hand shaking he sat on the end of the bed and reached for a tissue to stem the bleeding. He felt along the bedside table for his torch, kept there for emergencies. He almost laughed, as incidents such as this were far from his mind when he had bought the thing not long after moving in. He was comforted to find that it worked, its narrow beam of light showing that the cut had almost stopped bleeding. He was now aware that the garden was once more basked in moonlight and the clouds were moving again.

Slowly he regained his composure, pulse returned to normal and a sticking plaster, found by torchlight, covered the injured knee. Suddenly he felt very weary and lay on the bed closing his eyes for just a moment.

He awoke with a start.

'Please replace the handset and try again.'

The telephone repeated its monotonous message once more. Leaning over he did as instructed and picked up the offending piece of plastic from where it lay on the pillow, what was it doing there? More to the point he wondered, slowly coming to, why had he overslept? A glance at the clock radio, its digits flashing, provided the answer: it had obviously stopped during the night.

He flicked the radio switch over to manual.

'Eight-thirty on Thursday morning, here are the main points of the news, Sussex police are investigating several reports of UFO sightings near the coast at Chichester last night. Meanwhile the Prime Minister will today visit...' The announcer's voice tailed off as James rushed into the bathroom trying to make up lost time. He washed quickly, deciding to take his battery razor and shave on the train. Unidentified flying objects, what rubbish would they come up with next?

Hurriedly dressing he decided there was just time to change the plaster on his knee before leaving the cottage. He must be getting forgetful in his old age, as he was blowed if he could remember how it had been cut in the first place!

Blossom Time

by

John Allen

The last committee meeting before the Summer Flower Show was in crisis.

Jack Beeching, the village spokesman on such occasions, had been tanking up on bitter for the past two hours. Now, squeezed into the little room next to the bar parlour, fittingly called 'The Snug', his face was turning to flaming aubergine - a sure sign that he was ready to hold forth.

Impatiently he waited for the minutes of the last meeting to be read and approved. As soon as they were signed, he rose somewhat unsteadily to his feet and made his pronouncement.

'Perhaps I didn't ought to say this, Colonel Hardwick being sort o' gentry, but he didn't ought to have entered his whats-a-name in Joe's class... and him only just come here. I'm sorry Vicar, but that's how I feel and I think I speak for the whole village.'

He sat down to a chorus of 'Here! Here!'

The Reverend Gibbings shuffled his feet nervously. He was one of the old school and never found it easy to go into a Pub - let alone associate with drinkers. However, mixing with sinners seemed to be expected of him nowadays and so he complied. He took a sip of lemonade and wished for the hundredth time he had never accepted the Chairmanship. But he was something of a plant expert and so felt it his duty when asked to accept the task.

He rose to his feet, his hand by habit feeling for the pulpit rail, then, disappointed, continued up to his throat and tugged at his collar which had suddenly grown tight.

'Er... I take it by whats-a-name, Jack, you mean the Estocarium Whilhemtosa. I must admit I had never heard of it, but I'm afraid... er I mean... it does qualify for the Exotic Section... and Colonel Hardwick has every right... he was sent an entry form.

'I rang my cousin, George, at Kew Gardens and he was very impressed. Said it is a very rare Succulent from Africa - only found in elephant country where its camouflage as a piece of... er... er elephant's droppings makes it extremely difficult to find.'

'He admitted that they haven't even one at Kew... not at the moment. Any rate, he's coming down with some friends to see it as it might well be the only one in Britain. I don't know what to do about Joe though - I know he always wins this section.'

The vicar flopped down in his chair, gulped some more soft drink and mopped his brow.

Joe's continuing success was not surprising as for years his Epiphyllums had been the only entrants. No one ever objected to this kindly farce as Joe was crippled with arthritis and, at eight-four, was the second oldest inhabitant of the village. In the past he had filled every post on the Committee and won a First in every section.

Some of the Committee were of the opinion that the shock of competition might well be the end of Joe, and yet they hadn't the right to refuse the Colonel's entry, especially as it was to bring extra visitors and outside money into the village.

For a while there was an uneasy silence, apart from the slurping of beer and few muffled burps.

Then Mr Smart - Headmaster of the Primary School - rose to his feet. He was a pompous five foot nothing man and spoke slowly as if every word he uttered was a precious gem.

With the air of one about to outshine the Judgement of Solomon, he addressed the Committee as if they were his class of infants.

'It's quite simple,' he drawled 'bearing in mind this *Is* a Flower Show and Mr Joe Purvis's Epiphyllums bear magnificent blooms; all you've got to do, Reverend, is to praise the rarity of the Colonel's Whilhelmtosa, thank him for letting us see it - and then award the First Prize to Purvis. After all, a heap of elephant's excrement isn't everybody's cup of tea. Eh! What!'

Having thus solved the problem, Mr Smart sat down.

He received a ripple of applause, many nods of approval accompanied by numerous chuckles.

The Vicar smiled wanly, muttered something about must be fair and from force of habit, said 'Amen.'

After a few further details were sorted out, the meeting closed with everybody feeling they had handled a tricky situation with great aplomb.

Two weeks later, on the eve of the Show, many helpers erected the old and long-suffering Marquee. Nobody remembered how it had been acquired but there were many lurid stories about Wicked Squires... village maidens and an early example of appeasement. Putting it up was generally accepted as thirsty work and even those married to 'scolds' got off lightly for being excessively dry.

By the evening the 'big top' was up, the trestles in position and the entries all displayed in their respective classes. The little white cards, bearing the owners' names were neatly lined up like tombstones which had been whitewashed.

Joe, a bit apprehensive at the news of a rival, made a late night visit to view the Estocarium. He was so tickled when he saw it that he choked laughing and had to be thumped on the back. When he recovered, he sniffed at the little brown mound and stated to all and sundry that it didn't even smell like 'muck'. Then, so amused by his own wit, he choked again and had to be carried into the 'Magpie' and revived with brandy.

During the night there was a thunderstorm. The torrential rain battered the old Marquee and found out the weak spots. First drops and then tiny rivulets began to descend on the trestles. It had happened before, but nobody minded as it had the effect of freshening up the exhibits. The Exotic Section didn't escape and both plants received a minor drenching.

By morning the sky was clear and the sun rose in all its midsummer power. Soon a cloud of steam was rising from the huge tent. Inside the temperature rose sharply.

Around nine o'clock the officials arrived and made their round to see that everything was in order. On passing the Exotic Section one of them noticed that Estocarium looked different. On closer examination, from the very centre a small thin stalk was rising crowned with an oval knob.

An hour later, it was six inches long, what was now obviously a bud, was swelling visibly.

The Reverend Gibbings was hurriedly summoned. After one look, he threw up his hands in dismay and hastily retreated to the church. There, kneeling before the altar, he prayed fervently for the bud not to open before two-thirty-five pm as the judging took place at two-thirty.

By two o'clock the stalk was a towering two feet, the bud was now the size of a lemon and its tip was suffused with all the colours of the rainbow - a promise of the dazzling beauty to come.

Joe was sitting by his entry bestowing withering glances, all to no avail, at the gaudy interloper.

By now the outside displays were deserted, so were all the other exhibits inside the Marquee - everybody was packed in a tight circle round the scene of the drama and it looked to all the world as if an old time prize fight was taking place. For word had travelled with the speed of a prairie fire, that a long-standing tradition was about to go.

As the time drew near for the Great Judgement, an awed silence prevailed.

Suddenly the silence was shattered as someone exclaimed.

'It's the Colonel!'

The crowd parted like the Red Sea before Moses.

Unaware of the preceding drama, Colonel Hardwick ambled smiling towards the Exotic Section. The moment he saw his Estocarium on the point of blooming, he stopped in his tracks like one of the many elephants he had shot. He let out a snort which was almost a trumpet and, to everybody's amazement, charged at his plant. He snatched it up and stormed out of the Marquee and was not seen again that day.

Joe received his award with much less than usual assurance and announced that it was the last time he was entering for this class, as he felt he should make room for a younger person.

The following day, the Chairman of the Flower Show Committee received a letter from the Colonel.

It accused the Committee of criminal irresponsibility in using a worn out Marquee to house the exhibits, of gross incompetence for allowing his Estocarium to receive a soaking and further, of crass ignorance for not knowing that when an Estocarium Whilhelmtosa flowers - it dies.

Burning Ambition

by

Piers Manser

Dusk gathered around the houses of the small town and soon the trees were enveloped by darkness. Against the remnants of an October sunset the silhouette of a tall boy appeared. Tall and thin with wide shoulders and long legs, wide shoulders that now began to ache. The feeling creeping across his muscles like an incoming tide, the webbing of the thirty-five kilo bag of papers digging deep into his flesh, only halted by those broad (now painful) Scapula bones.

Soon a new source of pain and discomfort was discovered, a second blight on his ability to successfully walk straight. This fresh punishment was the progressive bumping of the paper-bag as its luminous surface ricocheted off his hip. Another tiresome bony place that he guessed would suffer even more badly by the next morning.

The 'Normany Post' was one of the two so called 'Free Papers' in the Town. The only revenue it gained was through advertising so the reporting remained gritty, the journalists obviously realising the real limits of the papers importance as far as news was concerned. But whatever it contained it had to be delivered and in a town where part time jobs were scarce - really more extinct than scarce - there the paper would find its distributors.

The money was lousy and the working conditions unpredictable, but it was cash and this distributor could still see the Silver Pearl sitting in its showroom, spotlights causing the perfectly formed high-hats to sparkle, the tension on the snare anxious for a healthy pounding. So it remained there, illuminated and alarmed, several thousand papers away but still possibly within reach. Not worth the effort in his friends view, not worth the effort in his parents view ('But at least he's doing something productive' echoed his mother's voice while his father sat and smirked). In his sights it was worth the effort and the pain... but how much pain?

The last house on the street was actually about one third of a mile away from the road; perched on the edge of what was the beginning of Roman Hill. Hidden by tall hedges it looked a lonely dwelling, the residence of a rich eccentric or a mad scientist. No one ever delivered to this house anymore. Its emptiness had been evident for years and the people in the street chose to ignore it, as it is best to ignore the peculiar things, those places that trouble your thoughts. Its usually wise to hurry along, thinking about food or work or home, anything but the thing that towers above you.

He knew none of this of course. This vital information was lacking from his inexperienced mind as he strolled (or rather staggered) up the steep overgrown path. He felt it though, felt it but didn't understand, and so he continued through the semi-darkness.

Reaching into the now depleted stock of papers he drew one automatically. Even though this was his first round he had learnt to withdraw, fold and clutch the paper without even thinking about it. His mind was in the Music Studio and he considered the numbers on the price tag gradually getting smaller. Whittled away by copies of the 'Normany Post', figures like those of a milometer running backwards. Figures that would eventually show triple zero.

Lifting the heavy iron letter box with one hand he thrust the paper through with the other, as he had done one-hundred and twenty times previously today. Suddenly however something prevented its entry, the newsprint crumpled and adverts started to tear. Frustrated he pushed with his remaining strength, straining until it gave way and the paper shot through. His hand unfortunately followed and disappeared into the opening. As quickly as it went through, jaws clamped down on it and jolts of agony reverberated up the thin boys arm.

Confusion struck him and he stood there for a few moments, questioning the reality of what had just happened. The blood was real enough however, and so was the pain. Something the other side of the door had attached itself to his hand.

The pressure of rows of sharp teeth pinned his fingers together, bone against bone, all coated in his own pure blood.

Pulling away was no use, it just increased the torture, causing him to see flashes of light as he closed his tired eyes.

And so he crouched there, part of him outside, less of him inside. That less was gradually becoming more as the thing on the other side pulled harder, his arm up to his elbow now soaked in a warm fluid he could only presume was his own. More and more of it flowed, precious liquid he only now really appreciated.

The night wore on, his screams for help resulting in a throat that could only rasp, the aching of the back of his mouth only rivalled by that of his arm. Surprisingly the only part of his trapped limb that hurt intensely now was the area that was pushed against the cold metal of the letterbox. He was sickened by the thought of what remained of his hand on the other side of the door.

Clouds chased across the moon's radiant face and soon scattered stars shimmered in a frosty autumnal sky. The grass soon glistened with a thin film of ice. The only sounds were the long slow breaths of the creature inside the house that had ensnared him. Sounds the boy no longer heard his battered sanity having finally crumbled. In one night he had gone through his short life, reminiscing, clutching on to what were left of good memories. He perceived himself now as only a memory in the lives of those that loved him and slowly he worked determinedly on his last task, the extreme effort producing a quantity of perspiration that soaked his clothes.

The first person to see the Great Fire of Roman Hill ignored it. Her drunken stupor caused her to break the heel of her brand new 'Next' shoes. A far more important cause for concern than the orange flames which had now swallowed part of the town.

Hours of effort had produced a match from the back pocket of his Levis, the use of only one hand had considerably slowed his work down but had not stopped him. His fatigue had deepened and lighting proved difficult but stubborn copies of the 'Normany Post' had finally flared into dry heat and a cruel fire that swiftly ate away at the rotting timber in the building's structure.

Soon five fire department trucks screamed towards the bright inferno, only beaten by an early milkman who never spoke to anyone afterwards about the sounds he heard from the fiery house. Sounds that haunted his dreams, sounds of laughter, wild laughter competing against the shrill whine of something that wasn't a dog but certainly didn't resemble anything human.

The next morning some came to see the smouldering mound that remained, others ignored and some, some had the time to complain. To moan about the late delivery of their 'Post' and to exclaim over coffee and cornflakes that 'something ought to be done about that new paperboy.'

The Twilight Rebel

by

Pauline Till

Jenny poured herself a cup of tea and sank into the huge comfortable armchair. She breathed a sigh of relief as she gazed through the french windows which led out to the beautiful grounds of Highbury Hall. Jenny and her husband Alex had lived here for the past five years. It was the perfect setting for a best-selling author to work in and Alex was writing exceptionally well just now. He was visiting London today, promoting his latest book but she wished he was here to share her relief.

Although Jenny was forty-six years old she remained extremely youthful. Her short brown hair framed an oval face with flawless complexion and dark brown eyes. The birth of her twin sons Jeremy and Matthew, now twelve years old, had done nothing to spoil the tall slim body, which looked as good now as the day she married Alex fifteen years ago.

After the sudden death of her widowed mother last year, Jenny had kept in touch with her mother's older sister Sarah. She had always been the rebel of the family and in her youth had been an excellent show-jumper. Sadly, last April she had suffered a stroke and this had completely changed her personality. The lively, amusing and extrovert aunt she once knew had suddenly become aggressive and occasionally violent. This had caused Jenny endless problems when trying to find a suitable Nursing Home to care for her.

Today was Thursday, third of October, and it was only three days ago that Jenny had left the Upway Lodge Nursing Home feeling satisfied that she had at last found the perfect place for her aunt to stay. Upway Lodge was built in beautiful surroundings and from her aunt's bedroom window she could see the horses in the adjoining field. This had pleased the old lady and Jenny had left her sitting by the window smiling at the scene below.

Sarah Birken was now seventy-eight years old, and since her stroke could only walk with the aid of a walking frame. Although she was only of medium height she still carried her head high, chin out, and wore her snow white hair in a french knot, which made her appear taller. Despite her physical disability she was still an attractive woman. During her eventful life she had encountered numerous men but had never married.

Jenny sipped her tea and thought of the surprise telephone call she had received early Thursday morning. Now she could smile, but at the time she had not been amused. She had begun preparing breakfast when the telephone rang.

'Mrs Thompson?' said a very agitated voice.

'Yes,' replied Jenny.

'This is Matron at Upway Lodge, please can you come immediately? Miss Birken is causing trouble and says she will only speak to you as she doesn't like it here and is threatening the other residents.'

Jenny apologised profusely and said she would be there as soon as possible.

The door was opened by Matron, a lady of mature years and bulky stature, wearing an expression of exasperation.

'Come in, Mrs Thompson,' she said sternly, 'I'm afraid Miss Birken has caused chaos here this morning and unless her behaviour improves immediately, I will have to insist you remove her today!'

Jenny's heart sank as she once again apologised. Matron led her along the corridor towards the Dining Room and she noticed several members of staff scurrying round from room to room holding what appeared to be false teeth containers.

As they approached the door leading into the Dining Room the sound of raised voices and clashing metal could be heard. On entering the room Jenny could hardly believe her eyes. There was her aunt seated by a table, brandishing her walking frame at the elderly lady beside her who was attempting to retaliate. Meanwhile, a nurse was restraining the gentleman sitting opposite from throwing the marmalade pot at Aunt Sarah. Squeals and screams of abuse were coming from the two fighting females while several other residents were banging their fists on the tables, urging them on! Bedlam reigned and Matron and Jenny rushed forward to help other staff who were now trying to control the dynamic duo.

'Aunt Sarah!' exclaimed Jenny, 'Stop that at once. What do you think you are doing?'

Her aunt was so surprised to see Jenny she put down the walking frame. Then, with a look of indignation she retorted, 'That woman didn't eat her toast and when I took it she snatched it back. Why shouldn't I eat it if she doesn't want it?' This remark made her opponent see red and she screamed,

'I'm waiting for nurse to find my teeth, then I'm going to eat it!'

Matron intervened and two nurses assisted the weeping, toothless resident out of the room, comforting her and assuring her they would find the illusive teeth.

Jenny sat down beside Aunt Sarah who began eating the piece of toast, with a look of great satisfaction. Peace was returning to the room and breakfast continued.

Matron asked Jenny to accompany her to the office where she informed her that Miss Birken had risen early and wandered round the rooms swapping everyone's false teeth containers. This had caused great distress to many as they tried desperately to put their teeth in comfortably.

After much pleading and general discussion it was agreed that they give Aunt Sarah another forty eight hours to settle in. When Jenny eventually left Upway Lodge two hours later, she hoped that her chat with the old lady had done some good.

On her return to Highbury Hall Jenny related the incident to Alex who listened attentively. When she had finished he thought for a moment and then suggested that it was possible a pet of some description may help Aunt Sarah to calm down. Obviously a cat or dog was out of the question, but they eventually decided to purchase a budgerigar. They knew Matron had allowed two other residents to keep birds in their rooms.

Later that afternoon Jenny arrived at Upway Lodge carrying the budgerigar in a cage.

'Please God, make this work.' She prayed as she entered the hallway.

Before reaching her aunt's room she met Matron.

'How have things been this afternoon?' She asked, observing the straight face before her.

'We did have one incident at lunch time.' Replied Matron. 'Miss Birken poured orange juice into Mrs Biggs' leek soup. When I asked her the reason why, she said Mrs Biggs had complained that it was too thick. However, nothing more has yet transpired.'

'Thank goodness,' sighed Jenny with relief. 'Is it alright for me to give Aunt Sarah this bird? We thought it may help to calm her down.'

'Yes, I see no reason why not. Colonel Forsyth has one very similar in his room. He is next door to your Aunt, maybe he will help her to care for it. The Colonel knows everything about budgerigars as he used to keep several aviaries,' said Matron with a little smile creeping across her face.

To Jenny's delight Aunt Sarah accepted the bird and decided to name it 'Bertie'. During her hour long visit she watched the two of them making friends and was pleased to see her aunt trying to get Bertie to sit on her finger.

Wednesday morning breakfast was over, the washing up done and Jenny was preparing to go shopping for a new dress to wear to a cocktail party on Saturday, when the telephone rang.

'Mrs Thompson,' said a familiar voice, 'I'm afraid we have had more trouble again this morning. Miss Birken decided to bring Bertie down to breakfast. Before anything could be done, he was flying around the Dining Room dive-bombing the residents, dipping his feet in their cereals and causing a great deal of mess. Unless you can make her control herself and the bird, she will have to go!'

'I'll be there immediately,' replied Jenny, slamming down the receiver and grabbing her coat.

By the time she arrived at the Nursing Home both Bertie and Aunt Sarah had been safely returned to their respective abodes.

Jenny decided to find Colonel Forsyth and ask for his help. He was an upright gentleman, very distinguished looking and most charming. He was recovering from a heart attack and she prayed that her aunt's behaviour would have no adverse effect on him.

The Colonel and Jenny sat with Aunt Sarah discussing how best to take care of Bertie and by the time she bid them farewell, they were chatting like two long lost friends.

'This time I think it's working,' said Jenny to herself as she drove home.

The whole of Thursday morning passed without the dreaded telephone call. It was time for afternoon visiting and as she entered Aunt Sarah's room she saw Colonel Forsyth and her aunt sitting together holding hands, talking to Bertie.

'Peace at last,' she sighed.

Jenny finished her cup of tea and smiled happily.

Amateurs

by

R J Edwards

At first, Mr Oxberry thought a branch had gone through the back window. Then he saw the large, unbroken sheet of glass thrown aside on the ground. And when he saw the suitcase next to it, his heart sank.

'Louise,' he called, 'I think you'd better come out here.'

There was a scrambling in the tent and Louise came outside. They were the only two awake on the camp-site this early on a Sunday morning. He heard his wife's whispered 'Oh, no' as she saw the scattered contents of the suitcase on the grass. Oxberry felt his own throat burning and his eyes prickling.

'But why? And right at the end of the holiday, too,' he asked.

'These things happen, dear,' she said, wiping her nose with a scrap of tissue. 'We'd better collect our things together.'

'What about the police? Should we move anything?'

'But it's all our clothes,' protested Louise. 'The dirty washing and everything, scattered around for everyone to see. Anyway,' she added practically, 'we have to see if anything is missing.'

'I suppose so,' agreed Oxberry, stooping to collect their belongings.

'I'll do this, dear,' Louise said. 'Is there any other damage to the car?'

Oxberry hadn't thought of that and went back to look.

'They've tried to force the lock on your door,' he called quietly, examining the dented and scratched lock. The attempt failed - 'which is why they took out the back window,' mused Mr Oxberry, out loud - but the lock was twisted and wouldn't open to the key. Oxberry walked back around the car to where the rear wiper blade was pointing drunkenly up at the early morning sky. He had the strangest feeling that someone, very close, had been listening, and laughing.

The camp-site owner tried to be helpful, but, as he pointed out, no other cars had been broken into, which was unusual in such cases. He repeated this several times, and it soon became clear that he would prefer to play the whole thing down. However, he agreed to inform the police.

Oxberry wandered back to the tent. Louise was waiting for him and at once he knew something was wrong.

'What is it?' he asked. Louise broke into tears, twisting her wedding ring around her finger.

'It's mother's bracelet,' said Louise. 'It's gone.'

'Gone,' repeated Oxberry. 'Are you sure?' The bracelet had once belonged to Oxberry's mother. He had inherited it, and when Louise and he had married it had been his wedding gift to her.

'I'm sorry, so sorry,' Louise kept repeating.

'But how?' asked Oxberry. 'We had the passports and money and things in the bag in the tent. Wasn't it with them?'

'Normally, yes,' replied Louise, 'but when we were out yesterday the safety chain broke and I was worried that I'd lose it. So I wrapped it in my hanky and put it in the pocket of my jacket. But it was warm yesterday evening and I left the coat in the boot of the car. I forgot about the bracelet, and now it's gone.

'Don,' continued Louise, 'I want to leave this place. Can't we pack up and go? I hate it here. And the lager louts have been giving me horrible looks.'

Oxberry knew who she meant. A group of teenagers was camped alongside. Generally, Oxberry like the young. He liked their energy and contrariness. But this group seemed to have no regard for anyone. Only last night Oxberry had had to ask them to turn the radio down and had been subjected to a stream of abuse. And they had watched him as he locked the car, carefully, as he always did. Anyone seeing that might not have appreciated that it was just his way.

'What sort of looks?' he asked.

'You'll see,' replied Louise. She had cleared up the mess by the car, and the kettle was boiling for breakfast. They settled down, at last, to eat. Several of the other campers stopped, as they passed, to express their sympathy, making a positive effort to say how sorry they were in English, as if to comfort them. The lager louts said nothing, though two of them at least were English. Except there were the looks. Every time that Oxberry looked up, one of them was looking at him, and then they smirked and giggled together. But it was while Oxberry was finishing his second cup of coffee and Louise had gone for a shower that it happened.

The lager louts were about to go out. One of the girls slowly unbuttoned her blouse as she walked to the car and then bent over the bonnet, licking her finger as if to rub a speck off the paintwork. Her breasts pushed against her opened blouse and a piece of jewellery on a thin cord around her neck swung forward into the open. Oxberry started forward, spilling his coffee. It was Louise's bracelet, he was sure of it. The girl smiled at his reaction, then pushed the jewellery away and slipped into the passenger seat, buttoning her blouse. The Renault pulled away. Oxberry could hear their laughter.

In the early evening the gendarme called. He was very sympathetic and listened to Oxberry's account, including what had happened that morning. He even went to question the lager louts.

'But, of course, monsieur, they deny everything. In fact - pardon me - the young lady says you kept staring at her breasts' - Oxberry reddened at this - 'and, unfortunately, no-one else saw what happened.' The policeman was young and well meaning and helped Oxberry make a temporary repair to his window to get him back to England, but when he had left their neighbours were smirking more than ever.

Oxberry lay in his sleeping bag later that night looking out at the stars. He was feeling his age, suddenly. The lager louts returned to camp quite early for them, though long after everyone else was asleep. The usual banging of doors made a baby cry farther along the tent lines, but after a while all was still. Oxberry gave it another half an hour and then slipped out of his sleeping bag. The moon was low but there was enough light for Oxberry to see what he was doing. He slipped the old washing up bowl into place and turned the tap. There was a slight noise as the viscous liquid ran out, but nothing more. Finally it was done. Oxberry collected the bowl carefully and shuffled away towards the toilets. Now there would be no sign.

The following morning they packed and had breakfast, sitting with their back to the car so that they did not have to see the smirking from next door. The lager louts were packing too, and set off just before Louise and Oxberry, laughing at them to the last. Oxberry followed sedately, tired but with a sense of anticipation. Eventually, Oxberry saw the sight he had been expecting. The Renault was parked by the side of the road, its bonnet up and four anguished faces staring at the engine.

'It's the lager louts,' said Louise. 'They seem to be in trouble.'

'Engine seized, I expect,' replied Oxberry, trying not to smile. 'Tends to happen if there's no oil.'

'What makes you say that?' asked Louise. Then she shot him a searching look. 'Don, what have you been up to?'

'Me, dear? Nothing.' This time he did smile, he couldn't help himself.

'By the way, Lou,' he added. 'This camping lark. Time we gave it a miss, don't you think? Stay in a hotel.' Louise gave a small sigh of relief.

'If you're sure, dear,' she replied.

'Yes,' said Oxberry. 'Stop in Lyon tonight, perhaps. Take a look in one or two of the antique shops. Thought we might find something for your birthday.'

Louise reached over and squeezed his arm, but she couldn't help saying: 'Don... Well, you were a long time when you went out to the toilet last night...'

This time Don smirked unashamedly. It wasn't the loss of the bracelet. That had simply upset him, especially for Louise's sake. It was the deliberate mockery. Too stupid to keep their petty crime a secret. Things had been tough after he'd left the army. What with the children to feed and everything. Thieving had been a way to pay the bills. But he'd never done any unnecessary damage - not like some of the young thugs today - and he'd always left the place tidy. It was bad enough having to steal from people, you didn't have to rub it in. That is what had angered him.

'Amateurs,' he growled. They had had to be taught a lesson.

The Debating Ordeal

by

Ella Mayes

A handful of us were waiting at the university bus stop on a freezing cold morning in January 1986. After what seemed an eternity, Patrick finally arrived in a minibus. He was to drive us to what would prove to be a most nerve-wracking public speaking ordeal - a debating competition in West London.

The plan was that six students would speak and the other two would offer moral support, which was what I had opted to do. However, only six students, turned up at the bus stop and I soon realised that I would have to take part in the 'ordeal,' the University of East Anglia (UEA) Debating Society was calling me in its hour of need.

We tried to discover what had happened to the two missing students. I rushed along the narrow concrete walkway to E block, to find one of the students, Robert, in bed with a nasty attack of gastro enteritis. Exercising his vocal cords would be out of the question.

Meanwhile, the other student had not yet surfaced. We believed that apathy was the problem there.

Our minibus soon left Norwich for the M11. Patrick, chairman, treasurer, membership officer and goodness knows what else of the debating society gave us our instructions. We were to debate the motion: 'This house believes that the age of consent should be lowered to thirteen.'

We would form three teams of two, with two teams speaking for the motion and once against.

We drew up our battle plans with which we intended to tackle the might of Oxbridge and other prestigious universities steeped in the long tradition of debating. The UEA Debating Society, however, had only been formed in October, an embarrassing three months ago. But Guy, Ian, Andrew, Patrick, Alex and I remained undeterred.

Ironically, Patrick who would speak against the motion with Andrew, was the only one of us who seemed to support it, for reasons best left to the imagination. The name of the debating game, however, was to set aside your own views and use your skills of persuasion to win hands down with a convincing argument.

We had to cope with Patrick's driving, heavy traffic fumes, the ill-effects of suspect beefburgers we ate from a roadside van and getting totally lose in West London before we eventually reached our destination, Royal Holloway College.

When we arrived, we discovered to our horror that we'd missed our free lunch. When originally trying to convince students to take part in this fearsome debating challenge, Patrick told us that at least we'd get a free meal. But we were too late.

The debating hour drew nearer. My partner, who also had the challenge unexpectedly sprung on him that morning, was more nervous than the rest of us put together. His full name was Alexander Quintin-Becksendale, barely eighteen years old. Patrick assigned the impossible task of trying to keep up Alex's morale to me.

What didn't exactly help was seeing all the other contestants, poshly clad in suits and dresses. The UEA teams looked, to put it mildly, somewhat scruffy. One of the opponents said to us, 'UEA, what on earth is that?' as if our precious university did not exist.

The debate would be conducted simultaneously in three different roms, with twelve teams of two in each.

Alex and I, the UEA B team, entered an imposing looking room to find we were unfortunately drawn against the Cambridge B team, which consisted of two rather aristocratic looking students. I discovered that I had to speak first out of the twenty-four victims.

My speech consisted of several arguments, including that the age of consent was low in other European countries and this operated very well there, that young people were now generally more mature and responsible at an earlier age. I stressed the strong importance of individual freedom.

At the end of the first minute you speak, other members of the team can butt in with 'points of information' to try to pick holes in the argument. When the minute was up, I was literally bombarded with points of information and tried to fend them off.

Then the rest of the students made their contributions. The most aristocratic one of the Cambridge B team was laughed at and made to look a prude as his 'against' argument didn't quite come off.

Halfway through the proceedings, it was Alex's turn. He was desperate for the toilet and announced: 'Ladies and gentlemen. Please may I be excused otherwise I am going to wreck the floor!' Alex stood up and walked out of the door.

I did not know which way to look as Alex's absence seemed an eternity. He returned to launch into what was a sensitive and thoughtful argument, but I reckoned we'd long since blown our chances.

In addition to the toilet incident, Alex had begun to vandalise his polystyrene cup by ripping it up into tiny pieces. I told him to 'stop it' as it would hardly create a good impression for the 'Hooray Henry' judges. But Alex did it all the more.

The debate continued as each speaker seemed to lay into previous speakers. I emerged largely unscathed until a trendy looking chap from the Brunel University team tried to tear my argument apart.

The debate was drawing to a close. The Bristol team consisted of a heavy-looking ginger-haired chap whose 'for' argument was extremely crude, but had the rest of us in fits of laughter.

The time arrived for the announcement of the winners. There were few surprises here, our crude friends from Bristol, our trendy friends from Brunel and our aristocratic friends from Cambridge.

Alex and I had blown it. So had both the other UEA teams.

Patrick had failed to impress the judges with his infamous 'supermarket trolley' argument. He suggested that lowering the age of consent would allow people to do whatever they pleased, regardless of the consequences. He said that the Government might as well wheel on a supermarket trolley of goodies or social reforms and keep piling more and more goodies in.

Where would it all end, he asked, his Welsh voice echoing around the room and sounding not unlike Neil Kinnock.

Disappointing though it was not to be preparing for the next round of debate, we knew we'd at least get home early. How wrong we were.

We first went to console ourselves in a pub near the college. At about eight pm, Patrick gave us a tour of the bright lights of West, then Central and finally East London. He took us to two pubs in Bethnal Green and then several of his friends' homes.

When the time was nearing one am, we suggested to Patrick: 'Hadn't we better start heading home,' knowing that East Anglia was a good few hours away.

However, the minibus had practically run out of petrol and we had to find a twenty four hour service station. We made a rather long detour and ended up in

Hertfordshire. As we cruised through Hertford at about two-thirty am, we knew there was a real danger of running out of petrol.

We finally did find a petrol station, but were still lost in deepest Hertfordshire by three-thirty am. I slept briefly then awoke to discover the minibus parked outside a police station with Patrick and Ian talking to an officer inside. What was going on?

It turned out that both of them were asking for directions, albeit a little late in the morning.

The minibus continued on its way, it was now about four am. Either the police officer had not given very good directions or they had not been understood, because Patrick still didn't know where we were going.

I was then horrified to discover that we were heading the wrong way down a dual carriageway, hastily put right by Patrick's U-turn.

After a few more muddled miles, we were suddenly stopped by a police car. A police officer approached Patrick, who wound down the window and it was then we realised that he might be over the limit, added to which he had not been wearing a seat belt. The officer wanted to know why Patrick had been driving so slowly. He explained that he was very lost.

This officer gave Patrick some foolproof directions and by about five am, we were finally heading for East Anglia. It was approximately five-thirty am that Patrick decided to subject us to his very worst jokes, which was rather unfair because there was no escape on this occasion.

After surviving the jokes, perhaps the worst part of this whole sorry escapade, I felt more awake and helped direct us back to Norwich. Never had arriving in that city been more welcome.

We finally approached the university campus at seven am. One thing was certain, not one member of the UEA A, B or C teams went anywhere near a lecture room on that day after the debate.

Idle Curiosity

by

David Topham

Had the wheelie bin moved? No. The small twig under one of the wheels was still there. Arthur had put it there three weeks ago - out of idle curiosity. Now, he was enthralled. He stared at the house: Number 3 Parnell Mews. Nothing had changed. The house stared blankly back. Hearing footsteps approaching, he began to move on. A tall girl smiled at him as she passed, a great dazzling smile. The shock almost caused him to collide with a lamp post. A door opened and closed. He looked round; the girl had disappeared. She must have gone into number 3; there was no other possibility. The high garden wall at the back obscured the ground floor. He stared up at the back bedroom windows. The grey curtains told him nothing.

While preparing his supper, Arthur was still thinking about number 3. He passed it four times a day: to and from work, and to his local, The Crown Inn. He had not even once before seen anyone going in or out. In the centre of a new development, surrounded on three sides by short terraces, number 3 was detached: that was the only unusual thing about it. For no special reason it had drawn his attention. There was no estate agent's board. He had even scanned the local papers for a private sale; there was nothing.

He usually went to The Crown at ten o'clock for one pint of bitter. Tonight he went an hour earlier, hoping for some new revelation about number 3. There was a light in the front bedroom! No curtains there. Arthur watched for twenty minutes, but there was no sign of movement.

That night he had trouble sleeping. It was the way the girl had smiled at him. Arthur knew that attractive young women do not smile at balding men of fifty without an ulterior motive. But what could that motive be? Dawn arrived: he felt completely washed out. He decided to ring the office and report migraine. The day ticked by in hours of fruitless speculation. Eventually he rang the office again, he urgently needed a few days of annual holiday. He had to break the bonds by staying away from number 3. Next morning, he set about spring-cleaning with manic ferocity and went to bed tired out. In spite of himself, at ten o'clock on the third evening, he put on his coat. He had already rationalised his actions. *It's stupid to let a house dominate my life: avoiding it is admitting it's important.* He repeated this resolve under his breath as he passed number 3 without a glance.

The Crown was packed; an engagement party. A young man reeled up and insisted on buying him a whisky. Arthur learned he was the groom-to-be. The drink went down too quickly. Reluctant to mix his drinks, he ordered another Scotch. By closing time there was a curious numbness in his fingertips.

He was almost past number 3 before realising it. There was light in the back window! A faint glow cast upwards from behind the wall. Caution blunted by the alcohol, he tried to pull himself up far enough to see over; but it was beyond his strength. He moved back round the front to the garden door. The catch was rusty; only by using both hands did he manage to lift it. The hinges squealed as he pushed. He stopped and held his breath. There was no moon. He had to rely on touch, putting out each foot tentatively. After what seemed like an hour he reached the edge of the building. Steeling himself, Arthur put his head slowly round the corner. The window was in fact a patio door; the room inside empty. A single unshaded bulb gave begrudging light. The furniture was sparse: three upright chairs, a sleeping bag on a sun-bed, and a small dining table. Beyond reasoning now, he gripped the handle of the window and pushed: it whispered open.

On the table was yesterday's Daily Mirror and the remains of a crude meal: a carton of milk and take-away containers. The air was thick with stale tobacco smoke. His foot nudged something; a cracked cup next to the sun-bed. It was crammed with dog-ends. The room began to swim. Turning, he stumbled to regain the freshness of the night.

Arthur woke late. For several minutes he lay completely disorientated: a giant hand seemed to be gripping the back of his neck. Marvel at his own daring gave way to terror when he imagined being caught. He would lose his job... His job! He was supposed to be in today! After ringing the office with another migraine, he sat at the kitchen table and wrote everything he knew about number 3 Parnell Mews. The previous night was difficult; without incriminating himself. He settled for hearing something and just looking through the window.

The desk sergeant coughed politely and leaned on the counter.
'What exactly is your complaint, sir?'
Arthur stared at him.
'I don't have any complaint. It's all there.'

The sergeant glanced at the pages in his hand. 'Yes,' he muttered, 'best if we take a look. Most probably squatters.' He folded the pages and put them in his breast pocket.

'But I will be informed?' insisted Arthur.

The sergeant stared at him for a moment. 'Well, yes. If you like, sir.'

Arthur went back to work the following morning. Passing number 3, he smiled. He had exorcised it. Returning in the evening, a new spring in his step, he noted with satisfaction that the wheelie bin had gone. As he was passing along the side of the house, the door opened behind him. Arthur stopped dead. The door slammed, and he heard the clicking of woman's heels moving away. He dashed back and peered round the corner. Though he could only see her back, he was certain it was her. She must have heard him because she suddenly stopped and looked back. He tried to turn away but could not. He was held by that beautiful smile. Then without a word she continued on her way. His mind full of new questions, Arthur rushed to a nearby telephone box. By the time he was connected, he was beside himself.

'Yes sir, how can I help you?' It was the same officer.

'Do you know about the Parnell Mews case?' demanded Arthur.

'You the gentleman that came in?'

'That's right. Something else has happened since you were there!'

'How do you mean, sir?' The officer sounded puzzled.

'The girl's been back!' Arthur shouted.

'Steady now, sir,' said the sergeant evenly, 'we haven't been yet. Look, don't worry, I'll get someone there straight away.'

'And you'll keep me informed?' insisted Arthur.

The officer sighed audibly. 'Yes, sir, we'll keep you informed.'

Arthur passed another sleepless night. Nothing he could imagine was able to reconcile the girl's open, friendly smile with the grimy interior of the house. After phoning in sick yet again, he sat beside the telephone, waiting for it to ring. At two o'clock his patience ran out: he dialled again.

'Yes, sir,' the sergeant sighed, 'I've had somebody round there. Nothing to worry about. It is in the hands of agents, apparently, McCarthy's. There's no sign outside for fear of attracting vandals and snoopers.' He could not help emphasising the last word.

'But what about the sleeping bag - the meal - and the girl?'

'Nothing there at all: place is completely empty. And the girl was from McCarthy's. Just spoken to her, matter of fact. Good day now, sir.'

Arthur sat gazing at the buzzing mouthpiece in his hand. Replacing it, he began to bang his head deliberately against the kitchen door-post.

In McCarthy's Estate Agency, a tall attractive girl answered the telephone.

'Is that you Theresa?'

She gave a start as she recognised the soft Dublin accent. Looking round at her colleague at the next desk, she kept her voice brisk.

'Yes, How may I help you?'

'You managed to get the place cleared, did you?'

'Yes, there's no problem now, sir.'

She smiled at a young couple coming into the office.

'The hell there's no problem!' hissed the voice, 'Now we've got to set up everything somewhere else - and find a new cache for the gelly!'

Theresa's smile grew brighter. She motioned the couple to sit down.

'Don't worry, sir, I'm sure I can come up with something suitable. Oh, and the other gentleman who was interested. Do you remember, the one I told you about? Well, he's - he's backing out. I'm sending someone to see him. Thank you for calling.'

Arthur was bathing his bleeding forehead when the door bell rang. He began to think of excuses for his appearance.

The Journey

by

Maureen Cox

It all began with a phone call late one Sunday afternoon in early December. 'Met forecast a gap of several hours on Tuesday between the present cold front and another following. It might be worth a trip to Ipswich.' Phil's young voice left a question mark in the air. My heart missed a beat: after waiting two weeks for the weather to improve it was obviously now or next Spring as far as the Western Isles were concerned. Not that the weather was our only consideration; a grass runway and long spells of rain could make a landing impossible. Still, the faintest opportunity could not be missed, so promising Phil I'd call in at Ipswich Airport the following morning, I put the phone down. My mind leaping ahead, I began planning the more mundane details of transporting an elderly, disabled man from hospital to the Isle of Mull with the minimum of disturbance and as quickly as possible.

Numerous phone calls were made back and forth, alternative arrangements had to be considered, the hospital alerted and so on. My mind was in a whirl that night as I tried to sleep and my fears justly founded as next day Phil, our intended pilot, handed me the weather forecast.

'Bad news I'm afraid, the front is moving much faster than anticipated and is most likely to appear around nine am on Tuesday. Even if conditions had held,' he continued, 'Mull is definitely out due to the airstrip being waterlogged.'

In view of the impending weather I was not sure of Plan Two either. However tickets were booked on an airline from Heathrow to Glasgow, also a helicopter standing by for immediate departure; with any luck that part of the journey would only take half an hour.

Father, still enjoying a leisurely breakfast when I arrived early next morning, was totally unconcerned, but a little puzzled as to why he was eating alone. I reminded him for the hundredth time of his impending journey. The resultant grin brought comments from the staff. 'That's the first time you've smiled since you've been here!' Somehow I squeezed his clothes, an old alarm clock, oddments from a hospital sale, doctor's letter, medication and a prepared hypodermic needle into four small, shabby suitcases. The journey began as we made our way down lengthy corridors to cries of, 'Good luck, Happy landings,' and 'Enjoy yourself.'

The two hour journey to Heathrow though uneventful, was frustrating as we neared our first destination. But before too long we were in the departure lounge with five minutes to spare. Long enough for a cup of tea, I thought, but the hot liquid had barely touched my lips when two hefty young men stood over us.

'Ready for your lift sir?' one said. Having waited three hours for his cuppa father would not be denied; his answer was to pour the precious liquid into a saucer and gulp it back with relish. Only then would he allow himself to be removed from the wheelchair into an apparatus for lifting him up the aircraft steps. He looked small, frail and helpless, a carpet slipper on his swollen foot and the empty trouser leg flapping as he was hurried along.

'Where is it I'm going?' he asked again as I wrapped a blanket around him and tightened his safety strap. That question unnerved me every time, but he was always pleased with the answer, saying, 'That's right, that's right.' Once more I wondered whether I had only dreamt of the conversation we'd had over the past few weeks as to where he would like to spend his last days. I shook the idea from my mind, no point having misgiving now, we had come too far. The family home was sold, contents disposed of, childhood memories packed in charity bags or sent to the town dump. Part of my life, all of his. What's it all about anyway?

The DC9 gathered speed, easily rising from ground to air; buildings vanished from sight replaced by an eerie cotton wool carpet and brilliant sunshine. Father was enjoying himself.

'A sweet sir?' The stewardess was pretty. A book, a drink from the bar, a snack, two cups of tea and another sweet all crammed into one hour and ten minutes. How do they manage it?

All too soon the lifting procedure began again and before many minutes had passed we were in an ambulance on our way towards the helicopter. That's when I noticed the rain was heavy and the cloud low. Phil had warned us correctly, the cold front had become well and truly established. Glasgow, I remembered, was often grey and wet, but the men who struggled to lift Father high above their shoulders were cheerful. The wind snatched at their words distorting them, causing the old man to cry, 'Eh, eh, what's that you say?'

The Squirrel's pilot completed his checks, the great rotary blades began to turn, slowly at first, pace gradually quickening as we rose upward and on. That's the road into Paisley - there's the R.O.F. - Michael's friend lived there and... Father gripped my arm scaring me, but he was alright. This was a day of new experiences for him: he looked young again, his eyes sparkling. At eighty three he had never flown before. I prayed his heart would stand the strain.

I had forgotten how beautiful Scotland in Autumn can be; craggy hills covered in shades of russet, brown and green, lochs, grey now reflecting heavy skies and rich, dark firs interspersed with sepia tracks. Derelict stone crofters' homes disappeared beneath us. A castle cold and forbidding stood high above all else, like a sentinel keeping watch. Clouds enveloped the scene; we descended again sending sheep scattering in all directions.

Gradually there was less land and more and more water. White crested waves peaked, toppled and crashed against rocky islands. On one more lush the only signs of life were a few sheep. Did someone visit every so often or had they been left forever forgotten?

We seemed to hug these tiny islands as though the pilot preferred to see some sight of land, however inhospitable. Winds buffeted our small craft making me very much aware of its frailty and insignificant efforts to survive nature's vindictive moods. If she were so inclined our destruction would be equally insignificant. Sea and cloud merged into one, nothing but greyness everywhere and torrential rain lashing against perspex and metal. Still the blades continued to turn.

Father nudged me, 'When will we be there?'

According to my watch we were half an hour overdue. I pictured my sister sick with worry, 'Not long now,' I said. Liar, I thought trying to guess where we were. Then suddenly, as if by magic, island, bay, boats and cottages sprung into view, and shortly after school house, playing field, ambulance, car and sister. Even from that distance I knew she was crying, the hanky fluttering from her hand as she waved frantically.

He asked me again, 'Where is this place?'

'Mull, Father, you remember, your home will be with Shirley now.' He smiled, content with my reply.

I kissed him goodbye wondering whether I would ever see him again, and knowing, for him, the journey was already forgotten.

Injured Parties

by

Gloria Smith

Sergio looked up from his book and glanced across at Clara faithfully mending a tear in his jeans. If she could only have known the drift of her husband's thought she might have applied herself less diligently to her handiwork.

For it had just crossed his mind that, if he had to, he could quite as easily settle down with someone else.

Clara gave her husband a quick glance as she sewed. He was obviously feeling warm and cosy from the wine at lunch, and in this vaguely happy state had nodded off - satisfied his wife had never looked at another man.

When he awoke, she was no longer in the room. He glanced at his watch. It was long past suppertime. He got up and went kitchenwards. The table was laid for one. Propped up against the pepperpot was a pristine note. It simply said: 'Ciao'.

A glance in the bedroom confirmed his worst fears - an empty open wardrobe, suggesting an impromptu flit and a deserted husband, who just had to drive round in pursuit in order to avoid being a laughing stock. But on opening the garage door he turned to stone, for where the jaguar had been there was merely a concrete space. When had she ever shown any inclination to learn to drive? Worse was the thought that it might be someone else at the wheel! He would ring Cosimo and cry out his anguish to a friend.

Shakily, he dialled the number. But it was Marina, Cosimo's wife, who answered the phone, blurting out between sobs of rage: 'Maschalzoni! I saw him pick her up at the corner - yes, Clara, your goody goody wife - she's run off with my husband!' came the deafening wail.

'Have you any idea where?' asked Sergio, already acclimatised to shocks.

'Yes - Brescolino,' and she recalled him to the holiday villa that she and Cosimo had purchased the Autumn before. The keys were definitely missing.

But would Cosimo take Clara to a place where Marina was known? That was just it - she wasn't. It was true she had stayed at the villa for a week to oversee some painting and decorating, but with Cosimo absent she had paid no social calls. Yes, Marina was sure that after that length of time, Clara could easily pass for Marina.

'Of course,' mused Sergio aloud, 'now I come to think of it, you two women are alike!' which did not endear him to Marina.

They decided to hire a car and go to the villa - confront their spouses, and even catch them in 'flagrant délit'.

It was late afternoon when they swept up the hillside to Brescolino, with Marina indicating the way along a country lane interspersed with villas. Suddenly, a raucous claxoning at the rear forced them to slow down to let a police car pass, followed by an ambulance, sirens adding to the din.

'We're close to the villa,' said Marina. And there it was round the next bend - but - how strange! With the police car and ambulance parked in the drive. As they stared over the hedge, they saw a casualty being brought out of the house - a blond masculine head just visible on the stretcher. Marina and Sergio looked at each other... Cosimo's hair was black.

When the ambulance sped out and past them Sergio could see into the garage. There stood his jag. Just waiting for him to reclaim it. He jumped for joy!

They parked down the road, and tip-toed through the open door of the villa, slipping into the front room out of sight of the kitchen from whence came a gabble of voices.

'Will the Signora kindly tell us what happened?' the police sergeant was heard to say.

Clara began her account - how her husband, as she referred to Cosimo, had gone to the village for provisions - how she had busied herself in the kitchen - and how she had suddenly been seized from behind... by this stranger... who had tried to kiss her... had declared his love for her... and recalled a passionate affair they had had in the Autumn, last year. And all the time - he was calling her Marina.

'Managia!' swore Marina from her hiding place.

'I struggled free,' went on Clara, 'Seized the nearest thing - a bottle - and hit him over the head with it. You know the rest, sergeant - I telephoned the police station.'

'Well you knocked him out, but you didn't kill him,' he said, with a hint in his voice that he thought it all a bit of a farce. Would they, as a matter of routine, produce their identity cards, please? Not really husband and wife. Hm...

So Cosimo jumped in with:

'My real wife was here last Autumn, alone, overseeing the painting and decorating - yes, *alone*. Her name is Marina.

'Alone?... Let us say, it was a case of mistaken identity... Signora, you must resemble the other lady quite considerably... It just remains for you to accompany me to the station to make a statement - for the books.'

Shepherded by the arm of the law, Clara and Cosimo passed within inches of their respective spouses.

Marina and Sergio ran to the garage. The keys were in the car, and it didn't take Sergio long to back it into the roadway and transfer their baggage to the boot. Then he left their hired car in the garage - and with a lipstick from Marina's vanity case, scrawled on the windscreen: 'Ring this number and they'll come and collect it.'

Settled in the car, both asked: 'What now?' Sergio eyed his companion up and down.

'It's not unusual for the injured parties to commiserate with one another,' he said.

After all, Marina had the advantage of Clara's looks, and her virtue was easy enough to allow his hand to transfer from the handbrake onto her thigh. It was this tacit agreement that sealed it, and sent Sergio speeding down the road in high humour.

He thought he'd adjusted well, all in all, by turning what could have been a minor tragedy into quite a promising interlude.

Child's Play

by

Pam Brown

David stood shivering with anticipation. The playground was filling up with rushed parents and querulous children, all swirling around like water in a filling bucket. He shifted his rucksack uneasily across his thin, hunched, shoulders. Would Tom come today? Would he be able to keep his promise? Please, if there was a God, make Tom come.

David looked around: he saw Emily's and Karen's mums chatting. Emily and Karen were both in his class. He watched them skipping with their matching ropes. Chloe's parents arrived breathless and laughing. Chloe held a bunch of daffodils. Her little brother had some too, although his were limp from being held so tightly. Chloe waved to David and her mum smiled at him. He wished his mum or dad would stay with him until the bell rang: it would be good to feel them standing near, but dad started work at six delivering cleaning materials, and mum dashed off to work as soon as she left him at the gates. He knew they had to work but they had always had time before, before Tom had died. Tom was his big brother and best friend. On a beautiful sunny day he had drowned in the canal. No one had known why, Tom was an excellent swimmer.

Since that day his parents had been distant, as though they were afraid to love David anymore because he might die too. Lost in their grief they were oblivious to David's sufferings and David was suffering terribly because since Tom had ceased to protect him, he was being bullied by Daniel. Daniel was a bright confident pleasant looking boy who killed other children. All the kids in David's year knew. No adult was aware of the terror inflicted on the pupil's by Daniel; subtle, terrifying, he left no marks unless the children told on him. Some of the children had tried to tell. Shelly had told her teacher and on the way home her brakes had failed when she was cycling down the big hill. Shelly went to a special school now. Joe had complained to the Dinner Staff. That afternoon he had fallen from the top of the wall bars in the gym. Well, he had thrown himself off when the teacher had been distracted. The children knew that Joe hated heights and never climbed up more than four bars normally. But the school had ceased to be normal anymore. Joe would walk again - eventually.

Last term a student teacher had sussed Daniel out. His motorbike had crashed headlong into a wall. The children had all bought flowers. Tiny Sarah had nearly made it to the Headmaster's office when a large dog had appeared as if from nowhere and attacked her. Everyone had been in school at the time so no one had seen exactly what had happened. Sarah had never regained consciousness to tell. Then Tom had been drowned. Daniel ruled OK?

It was during half term that Tom had told David what happened. How he had gone for a swim with his mates and how they had all held him down until he stopped struggling. They wouldn't remember but Tom remembered seeing Daniel on the lock gate, smiling with his eyes glowing weirdly in the sunlight.

David had been terrified when he first saw Tom, but once Tom had explained David knew that soon everything would be all right.

David watched the gate anxiously. Tom appeared, waved, gave the thumbs up sign, grinned and disappeared. David smiled, a proper smile as the bell rang and they all lined up.

Once Tom had reassured David they had a good laugh that night in bed as David told how the Headmaster had called a special assembly to announce the sad news that Daniel Carter had been killed; road accident, he said. They all prayed for his soul 'bit late', David thought, but bowed his head. Only the adults knew what had really happened and they shielded the children from the horrific details of Daniel's death. There had not been much of Daniel left after he had been sieved through the grill of a runaway truck on the big hill.

Tom said he'd always wanted to be a driver.

Tom gave David a hug and said he had to go now but he'd be keeping a watch on David, just in case.

Later David's mum came up and sat in the moonlight staring at her youngest son as though she had not seen him for a while. She tucked him in and kissed him gently. She hadn't done that for ages. David slept well.

No Time to Explain

by

Sue Edwards

Seated on the top deck of the bus Veronica had to rub the steamy windows with her gloved hand in order to see out. The lions at the foot of Nelson's Column looked as though they had been made of steel as they glistened in the dripping rain and as the bus, caught in the evening rush hour traffic, slowly weaved a way around Trafalgar Square she thought with a stab of annoyance of how tonight of all nights she had especially wanted to get home on time.

She did so want to set the scene before Derek got back from the office by preparing a romantic dinner for the two of them. She would light the candles, put on his favourite Mahler CD (well it was actually her favourite Mahler CD - Derek was not over keen on music but she was gradually teaching him!) She would have the wine at the right temperature and uncorked so that when he came through the front door she would be able to hand him a glass - all with a beautiful smile on her face as though nothing had happened. It all had to be perfect, for Veronica had come to an important decision. She was going to allow Derek to have a puppy dog - she was going to make the supreme sacrifice. The truth was that at this time she was prepared to do anything at all, to help revive a marriage that seemed to be heading towards being just another divorce statistic.

Derek was an unambitious man. He was so easy going that he had allowed Veronica through-out their marriage to always make the decisions. For him this was her very attraction. He had always admired her impeccable taste, her ability to make snap decisions which he was quite incapable of doing. He liked her careful choice of friends for he had none of his own - Veronica had seen to that and most of all he had been right behind her as she climbed ahead with her career. He was so proud of the fact that she was now a Director of the Finance Company where she had worked for the past ten years. He felt no envy what so ever that he had remained in a very junior position within the same company.

One thing, however, did upset him. Derek had always wanted a dog and Veronica had tried many times to explain the impracticalities of owning a dog when they both went out to work. He would never listen and had remained unmoveable on this point.

Actually it was Veronica who hated dogs - had always thought of them as dirty smelly creatures and they, seeming to sense her dislike of them, reciprocated by treating her with unfriendly suspicion.

It was after the terrible row that morning that warning bells began to sound in Veronica's head. She had never given any thought as to why Derek wanted a dog so badly but the clue lay in his statement as he had slammed out of the house.

'I loath you,' he had hissed through clenched teeth - 'I hate our life together - I hate this terrible house and most of all I hate being married to someone who is incapable of giving any love,' and as a final gesture he had picked up her favourite Meissan 'Swan Lady' from the hall table and hurled it against the wall breaking it beyond repair. The colour had drained from her face as she stood looking at him, her mouth open as though she was trying to say something. Her voice had become petrified in her throat and silent tears rolled down her cheek. She simply did not know how to react to Derek's unfamiliar behaviour. She had re-lived the argument all day - her preoccupation was noticed by her colleagues at work. She had churned the matter over and over in her mind until at last she had reached a compromise. If Derek would agree to keeping the dog in their garage she would be quite happy to go along with the idea.

Peering out of the bus window into the gloom, something caught her attention - a fleeting image - nothing more. An umbrella forced aside by the wind - lovers discovered in the intimacy of a kiss oblivious to the weather. A little white Jack Russell dog on a lead jumping about their feet. The sheeting rain reflecting in the orange glow of the street lamps intensified Veronica's feelings of alarm. As a sudden gust of wind hurled the rain against the bus window Veronica her head now throbbing from the smell of stale bodies and wet clothes ran down the steps of the bus - blind panic making her careless of the slippery surface. She had started the journey feeling so hopeful but now she was frightened.

She had to be sure but as she looked into the gloom the image had faded - vanished into a myriad of black umbrellas.

The lovers and the little dog passed the body that had fallen from the bus - too wrapped up in each other to care, but the little dog just for the briefest of moments stopped - his body all of a quiver, his ears pricked up. Giving a little bark it was as though he sensed the feeling of turmoil surrounding the dead girl but then losing interest he followed the couple into the night.

Bird of Paradise

by

Karen Martyn

Mike nodded a greeting to the barman and said 'How're things Ted?'

The man on the next stool shifted his weight and muttered 'Could be better', but remained hunched and staring across the bar. Mike exchanged a knowing look with the barman who nodded slowly in response to the unspoken question.

In the last few weeks, Ted had been drinking considerably more than his daily pint before the train. Fellow travellers on the seven-fifteen home to the suburbs, he and Mike knew each other by first names only and had barely skimmed the surface of their lives in conversation, yet over the months they had struck up a pleasant time passing acquaintance.

More recently, Mike had found himself in the role of involuntary confidante and had quite unintentionally, built up a picture of Teds somewhat sad existence. Once a dynamic figure in the city, it seemed that Ted had been shuffled aside in favour of younger men with razor sharp minds and tongues to match.

'One of them called me a dinosaur today,' he'd miserably informed Mike one evening, when the late arrival of the train had led to him becoming more intoxicated and morose than usual. Guessing Ted to be no more than forty-five, forty-eight at the most, Mike had felt a twinge of alarm: he was, after all, fifty himself next month.

Later that same evening, he had looked more closely in the mirror and wondered if, perhaps he should start drinking mineral water and dressing more snappily, maybe even join a gymnasium. Thoughts of his recent promotion to dizzying heights an adoring secretary and near sycophantic assistants, had come rushing to the fore and he had allowed his reflection a smug smile.

'Besides,' he thought now, with a flush of pleasure, 'I have Sandy.' Recently widowed, his new love was a fascinating combination of passionate demands and vulnerable helplessness, that Mike found irresistible. Smitten to the core, he only wished they could spend more than three evenings a week together; but had understood perfectly, when she'd looked at him with misty eyes and said in a tremulous voice 'I need time on my own to recover.'

He was decent enough to respect her grief and besides, as a recent divorce, he quite relished the excitement of a part-time love affair.

As for Ted; Mike glanced sideways at the other mans drooping profile and pitied him for not having a Sandy in his life. Ted rarely mentioned his wife without sounding disgruntled.

'She liked me when I was rich', he'd divulged in a moment of frank self-pity 'now she's out all the time, organising raffles and jumble sales with all her lady friends.' Then another time: 'Is it possible to get baked bean poisoning? I've had them on toast four times this week.' In Mike's imagination, the nameless, faceless wife had assumed the identity of a selfish, tweed-suited frump, who had obviously lost interest in her husband.

As if reading his thoughts, Ted mumbled dejectedly 'It's our anniversary today.'

Mike was unsure whether to congratulate or commiserate. 'That's nice,' he offered as a compromise. 'Are you celebrating tonight?'

The other man let out a loud guffaw, as if Mike had suggested abseiling naked down Big Ben. 'You must be joking,' he said bitterly, 'She's got some 'do' tonight, just for a change,' he added sarcastically. He affected a high pitched whine and went on 'Please understand Ted, it's a very important fund raising event, Lady So and so will be there.' He lapsed back into his own voice and continued glumly 'Never gets back till late, I'm always asleep.'

Mike looked at the freshly re-filled glass and guessed this was probably true.

Ted fumbled in his pocket and slammed something down on the bar.' Bought her this too, don't know why, bloody fool I must be!' Mike watched as the trembling fingers opened the blue velvet box to reveal a sparkling brooch.

'It's beautiful,' he gasped, genuinely impressed by the exquisite detail of diamonds intricately fashioned in the shape of a tropical bird. A dazzling combination of amethysts, emeralds, sapphires and rubies, formed the birds exotic plumage. 'Bird of Paradise', explained Ted, with a strong hint of irony.' Had it made specially, cost me the rest of my shares.' He sounded regretful about spending what must have been a considerable amount on the unique brooch, but Mike suspected that his regret was more about a sense of anticipated rejection than wasted money. In spite of everything, the poor man was still making an attempt to win back the love and affection of an undeserving wife.

They spent the journey home in unaccustomed silence, each one acknowledging the others need for private, and in Mike's case strangely depressed, thoughts. He hardly knew the other man, yet wished he could offer something in the way of consolation or encouragement. It was a shame to watch a fellow human being slowly destroy himself through lack of self esteem and the futility of unrequited love.

'It's very sad,' he said later that evening. He waited in his lounge with a drink, while Sandy spent time getting ready. She had arrived later than usual, a little dishevelled and breathless from rushing. 'Won't be long,' she'd promised flying into the bedroom in a flurry of coat and bags. 'I said it's very sad,' he repeated and guessed from her absent-minded 'mmm?' that Sandy was pre-occupied with applying lipstick.

'I wish I could do something for the poor man.'

'Who's that darling?'

She hadn't been listening to a word. Mike felt a sudden rush of anger, but reminded himself that there was no reason why she should be interested in his fellow commuter.

He wandered into the bedroom, where Sandy sat at the dressing table facing her reflection. He watched her pert figure straining against the black dress as she leaned forward to stroke colour on her curling lashes and wondered why he should let another mans misery spoil his evening.

'There, I'm done,' she announced, clipping on ear-rings and moving her head from side to side in obvious self-approval. She stood up slowly and turned to face Mike.

'Do I meet with your approval sir?' She asked, with a seductive turn of the hips.

She was a stunningly attractive woman for her age, which Mike knew was the wrong side of forty and had reason to be proud of her looks. But at that moment her unabashed vanity niggled at him. He chided himself for letting his downcast mood threaten the pleasure that lay ahead and pulling her to him gently kissed her scented neck.

'Oh darling!' Sandy exclaimed, 'I just remembered something.' She reached behind her and handed him a small box. 'I was left something in my aunts will. She was an old dear, very sweet and it's a beautiful thing but,' she pursed her lips in mock guilt and whispered 'I'd rather have the cash.' She looked at him with little girl lost eyes and continued 'Could you get it valued for me, I'm so useless at these things, but I do know it's very valuable'.

Mike paused for a moment, feeling a sudden chill of apprehension spread like iced water through his veins. As frightened to open the box as if it contained a deadly spider, he closed his eyes and slowly raised the lid. His eyes snapped open in cold disbelief, staring speechless at the glittering brooch he had admired just a few hours earlier. 'Bird of Paradise', he intoned in a voice flatwithshock. He looked at Sandy, realising her true identity, but seeing a stranger. 'Bird of Paradise,' he said again and closed the lid.

The Birthday

by

Anne Hoad

As the mists of sleep cleared slowly from her mind she woke to the fog of a dismal November day.

'It's my Birthday.'

There was no emotion in the remembrance. Just a cold ache. An ache that matched well the greyness and dullness of the month. It seemed to her fitting that she should have been born at such a time of year. It seemed no less appropriate that she should have been cursed with the sign of the Scorpion. A nasty, ugly, hostile insect which sulked around under rocks in dingy desert places and whipped up it's venomous tail to destroy the inquisitive, unsuspecting, and often innocent, passer-by. Yes, hate it as she did, the scorpion was appropriate for her. Yet she, like the creature of her birth sign, only wished to live in peace and be left alone to enjoy what sunshine might come her way.

There had been precious little of it in her life. Fifty years old and what had it meant? Born on a Saturday to work hard for a living. And she had.

She didn't eagerly wait for the postman. She knew that no-one would remember her special day. It was not that her two daughters were exactly indifferent but they had their own lives to live. They were busy and successful, due in no small part to the sacrifices she had made for them, and they were forgetful where she was concerned. She had parted from their father many years earlier. Another reason that she did not expect the post to bring her any greeting was that she was, she knew, secretive about her birthday. Very few of her considerable number of friends knew her date of birth and few thought to ask. The cause of her secrecy had to do with innumerable hurts. If no-one knew her birthday, she unconsciously realised, she could not be disappointed if no greetings plopped quietly onto the doormat. Not that she didn't long to have cards. She did. No-one knew with what secret delight she received the one or two greetings from those who had penetrated her reserve well enough to discover her anniversary. No-one knew how she kept these tokens of affection locked away in a drawer, treasuring them.

It was not that she was not loved. It was that she could not quite believe herself loved.

Slowly she crept from her bed, quivering in the autumn chill. Pulling her wrap tightly around her ageing body she made her way down stairs and sleepily switched on the kettle for her ritual cup of tea. Rover, the dog, lazily watched her, idly wagging his tail, not moving from the warmth of his bed in the corner.

She drank her tea, allowing herself an extra wheatmeal biscuit as a concession to the celebration she wished for herself, and went through the necessary morning routine. She didn't consciously think about her birthday. She just accepted the sadness and the ache of the memories which it stirred deep within her soul. Birthdays had always been a source of pain to her since she started school and discovered that other children had special treats on their special days. It had gradually dawned on her that maybe her parents weren't really keen to remember how and when she had fought her way into their world, invading them with all the drama, the dependence, the growing curiosity, the essential demands of young life.

She had a memory, rarely disturbed, of a day at school.
'Who can tell me what's special about today?' the adored teacher had asked.
'How does she know it's my birthday?'
But, even as the thought passed through her mind the class was alive with excitement as one and another raised eager hands to tell the class that they knew it was bonfire night. And, amazed, she listened to the story of Guy Fawkes and his evil deeds. She was at a loss to understand why the day was celebrated, not fully grasping the truth that his capture and destruction caused such delight. But she did understand that the others in the class had fireworks and a bonfire and a party. She hurried home expecting no less and she could never understand the blank anger which greeted her eager enquiries. Sitting alone on her cold bedroom floor, playing with the toy tin tea service, which had been her birthday present, she pondered these things. The tea service delighted her. It was decorated with the willow pattern which she loved so much. She talked to her two dolls, faithful, loyal, constant and only companions, explaining her confusion to them. She heard fireworks booming in the distance. She rose, clambered onto the window sill and opened the window wide. She leaned out as far as she could, straining her neck to catch a glimpse of the wonders which her class mates and, it seemed, the whole of the rest of the population of the small town, were enjoying. She heard whoops and screams of delight but she could see nothing. Eventually she closed the window, disappointed, cold, lonely, sad. Gradually she built up in her mind, over the ensuing years, when, each

November the firework party (and any other kind of party) were denied, without explanation but with anger, her own explanation. She decided that she was mysteriously linked to Guy Fawkes in some way, and that if her parents were to risk allowing her to share in the general celebrations, she would be burnt on the fire like him. Perhaps it was her parents who fed her the idea, on order to silence her. In later years she thought this likely.

There was one memorable birthday. After the break up of her marriage one enterprising friend, having no knowledge of her Scorpion secret past, arranged with her small daughters to throw a party for her. All unsuspecting she had arrived after work for a meal to discover a party of close friends awaiting her. She was moved to tears.

'It's the first time I've ever had a birthday party!'

Her friend was astonished.

'But what about your twenty-first? You must have had a party then?'

'No. I was on duty all day. We were short of staff so I had to work a twelve hour shift. One of the patients found out it was my birthday and told Sister. She took me into the bathroom after the shift and gave me a Martini.' She laughed, 'Sister didn't know I didn't drink but I felt she'd be hurt if I refused, so I had it. But when I asked why she didn't have one with me she said she never drank, she just kept the bottle in the office for special occasions! Silly, isn't it?' She paused, the pain twisting like a knife in her as she saw the distress in her friend's face, so, as she always did, she laughed it off, 'That was my Twenty First birthday!'

Memories tucked away out of pain's reach... But today she did not dwell on memories. She did not dwell on the passing of fifty years nor on the secret dread of the ensuing inevitable decline. She had, after all, started a new job, just this week. Changing jobs was her way of challenging herself to greater and greater endeavours in order to keep her inner pain and loneliness at bay. So, on this grey November day, she showered and dressed carefully, as she always did. She took her friendly spaniel for a brisk but chilly walk, barely noticing her surroundings. She made her way with a mixture of enthusiasm and apprehension to her office. The new job was stimulating in itself. Her new colleagues were friendly enough. She was aware that they were still summing her up but she was confident about her work. It was the only thing she was truly confident about and she knew that, whatever her relationships at work might be, she would inevitably earn their respect for her professionalism. It was always so. She was respected but not loved. Love was what she yearned.

It was mid morning and work was well under way when the delivery came. The van drew into the car park outside her window marked 'Joanna's Flowers' and the young man opening the rear doors produced an enormous bouquet which he proceeded to carry into the building. She barely noticed. A few minutes later the flushed and smiling receptionist walked into the room.

'Just look at this glorious display,' she said, 'it's for you, Mary.'

'For me?!'

She was speechless. For a while she did not move. The receptionist came nearer. 'Yes. You must have a secret admirer. Aren't they lovely?'

Stunned Mary rose from her chair. It must be a mistake, surely, but she did not voice her doubts. Hesitantly, fearfully, lest the flowers were indeed for someone else, she moved to receive the bouquet. Feeling the smiling faces turned in interest towards her with trembling fingers she opened the little card attached to the cellophane wrapping.

'Happy Birthday Mum. We love you. Hope the new job is going well. With all our love, Jane and Sandy.'

A warm glow flooded her body lighting up her whole being. They hadn't forgotten after all. It was her birthday. She was, perhaps, loved after all. Maybe she would spend her second half century learning to believe it. She smiled at her new colleagues who were beaming at her.

'Oh, it's from my daughters. It's my birthday. Wasn't that sweet of them?' And she quietly went back to her work.

Outside the window a pale sun pierced the clouds of the grey November day.

Driven

by

Neil Davies

I knew this man. This young man. He was in love with a woman who worked in the same office as him. She was older than him. Good at her job. She had drive.

He worked hard too. He didn't have the same amount of experience as her but he was quiet and got on with his work the best he could.

But she distracted him. A lot. He loved to watch her, to hear her voice. He couldn't help it. He would get to work really early just so that he would be there for when she arrived. She would walk past his desk and smile at him as she went to her own, and just that smile would make him feel good inside all day. He didn't doubt that he loved her, but he didn't want to tell her. She was happily living together with someone else. They were not married but they were as good as, so he didn't feel that he had the right to go telling her that he loved her. He didn't have the right.

Yet he did love her. He knew that. During the moments that they had together when he could look at her and say silly things that would make her laugh, he was happier ... he was happier than he ever imagined he could be. Yet at the end of each day they would go their separate ways and his happiness would disappear with the setting sun. This went on for quite a while until at last he could no longer bear his predicament, being tossed from one emotion to another and then back again ... and so he handed in his resignation. He felt that if he didn't see her every day then perhaps he wouldn't think about her as much as he did. Perhaps he would be able to forget her.

She was sad to hear of his decision to leave the company and said that she hoped that they would be able to keep in touch. She meant it too. She had never flirted with him or led him on, but she had enjoyed his company and that was important to her.

His decision to leave had been pretty sudden and he didn't have another job to go to. Finding work was difficult. There was a recession and plenty of people were hungry for work. People who had more drive than him.

So he was out of a job and had time on his hands. Without work or activity to occupy his mind he found himself thinking about her more, rather than less. He couldn't stand it. He began to convince himself that maybe he had been wrong not to tell her how he felt about her. Perhaps it was right that she should be with him. After all, her boyfriend couldn't possibly love her as much as he did.

So he called her at work and they arranged to meet during her lunch hour. She was pleased to see him but could tell that something was troubling him. She asked what it was, and he told her that he loved her ... He told her that he loved her and he told her just how happy she made him feel. He complimented her upon her looks, her smile, her voice, her polite manner, and then he explained why he had left the company.

And she listened to his compliments and explanations until she could no longer permit herself to hear anymore. She had considered him a friend and now, I suppose, that friendship had been betrayed. She got up and left without saying goodbye.

For the next couple of days, he wandered around in a virtual daze. I don't even know where he went. He was confused, upset. He couldn't leave things as they were. He had to see her again to make sure that she was alright. He didn't want her to hate him for feeling the way that he did about her.

So he drove to her house that evening. Only, she didn't answer when he rang. Her boyfriend did and he was not pleased to see the young man. His girlfriend had been in bed for the last couple of days suffering from an acutely painful migraine. The boyfriend, who was normally a very friendly and likeable man, had established that her suffering had been caused by the young man. The boyfriend's anger led him to strike the young man when he saw him upon the doorstep. The young man was punched in the face until his nose and lips bled. He did nothing to defend himself and when he fell to the ground, he remained silent as he was kicked repeatedly in the stomach.

He lay on the ground for a while until he felt he was able to move. He then got up and began to walk away. He didn't look back or wonder if the woman that he loved might be looking at him from her window. He just walked to the car, got in, started the engine, and drove. He drove down the street and then on to the main road. He carried on driving until the street lamps of the town were no longer to be seen in his wing mirror and he was just driving into the night along roads that he did not know. When the sun rose the next morning, he was still driving away from the woman that he loved. There were tears in his eyes and when he coughed, specks of blood spattered the windscreen.

Billy's Dog

by

Tom Thompson

When we were quite young brother Billy and I, each with our sixpence, used to visit Wood Pie and Mash shop, where, for tuppence we carried our plate to the marble topped table to consume our meal.

Once, When we came out Billy walked over to the dog we had noticed earlier sitting on the edge of the pavement. Dirty and unkempt, it was sniffing aromatic meat-laden air. Billy of course has to pat the dog and ask it how it felt. Smelling the pie and mash on Billy's breath, the dog instantly fell in love with him.

Our usual Saturday morning treat and ritual was a meal followed by a cowboy film. Unfortunately the dog decided to accompany us to the cinema, and as Billy didn't want to lose his new friend he had the crazy idea of smuggling the dog into the cinema, so leaving me in the queue he walked round to the side door, returning a minute later without the dog.

Pushing and screaming and cheering, a few hundred junior mafia erupted into the building scrambling for seats. We put our coats on a seat between us as a reserved sign, and as the houselights dimmed and the advertisements appeared on the screen; Monk and Glass Custard Powder - Black Cat Cigarettes - Caleys Milk Chocolate - Fat Sam's Fish Shop, Billy disappeared and the next thing I am aware of is the dog sitting between the two of us, eyes already focused on the flickering screen.

Honestly, that dog sat through the film as entranced as the rest of us, watching Tom Mix halt the stampeding cattle, kill a few dozen cowboy villains, untie and rescue the maiden from the train-lines and finally ride off into the sunset. Amidst the cheers, and boos and whistles of the appreciative audience, not once did that dog bark to get us thrown out. Perhaps it was because he was eating more of our peanuts than we were. *The End*. Lights went up and clattering of spring loaded seats accompanied the crunching underfoot of peanut shells and sweet wrappers as we spewed out onto the street.

I asked Billy, 'How did you get the dog to wait for you at the side door?'

'It's an old countryman's trick,' he explained. 'If you let the dog have a good sniff at you and leave a bit of your clothing with it, he knows you will be back, and he just waits for you. I left my scarf.'

'I didn't know that,' I replied.

'I did,' said Billy - who had never spent a day in the country in all of his nine years.

On my way home, I said. 'What if dad says you can't keep him?' Was it jealously that prompted me to turn the screw a little and add, 'Bet dad kicks him out!'

Now the dog's eyes look troubled and I imagine he is thinking, 'I'm going to adopt Billy. I've been to the pictures, and had the best day of my life eating all those peanuts. I feel loved.'

When he sees the dog, dad shouts, '*Out*. Take that mongrel out of my house! I've got enough on my plate without feeding stray dogs too!'

Up to this point in time mum is all in favour of dog-eviction, but being a woman takes the view that if he stays 'no', then she says 'yes'.

Her arm draped over our shoulders, she attacks. 'I go to work too, and you don't exactly keep me you know. Anyway I don't suppose he'll eat much'.

'Oh I wont'. I won't,' barks the dog, re-appearing from beneath the table.

'Look he likes me. He's taken to me,' croons mum, wiping her dog-licked chin.

Dad signals the white flag by deciding to clear off to his local but his bald head won't let him go without cover.

'Where's my cap? Anyone seen my cap?'

'Find boy, find,' Billy instructs the dog, who bounds up the passage sniffing and scratching at the coal cupboard door.

'He's found your cap daddy.' Billy is triumphant.

'Well, well, so he has. Good dog that - he can stay.' This of course only confirms what mum had already decided.

The dog looks at Billy as if to say, 'Good job you put his cap under your armpit before you put it into the coal cupboard, otherwise I never would have found it!'

What a difference a week made. The dog had been washed, groomed and polished with mum's best hair brushes until it's coat shone like a copper kettle.

But now it was Sunday lunch-time.

'Go down to the pub and tell your dad dinner's on the table in twenty minutes,' orders mum.

Soon the three of us are peering round the door of the Timber carriage, and Billy calls, 'Dinner in twenty minutes, dad'.

Just to test what the effect would be, I elaborate. 'Mum says if you aren't home by then, you'll eat it cold'.

'Who's the guv'nor is your house, Charlie?'

'Drink up, Charlie.'

'Run along home then, Charlie.'

I'm quite pleased by the reaction and share in the general laughter.

'I'll be home when I'm good and ready,' growls dad and in an attempt at diverting attention points with his glass towards the dog. 'What about that, then!' and as all eyes focus on the dog, 'Here boy'.

The dog bounds into the pub and is quickly drinking best bitter someone had poured into a clean ash-tray. Slurp, slurp, and it was all gone.

'Likes his beer too Charlie. What's his name?'

'Never been able to make up our minds about that,' responds Charlie.

Now the dog is up on it's hind legs, front paws resting on the bar counter as if about to order another pint. The Timber Carriage landlord has got himself prepared and pouring half a pint over the dog's head, pronounces, 'I name this dog Timber.'

Alternatively sneezing and licking his lips the newly launched Timber retreats to the safety of the doorway.

Timber, Billy and I were having a marvellous time in the park, throwing sticks for each other, eating jam sandwiches and drinking home-made bright yellow lemonade.

Now lying on our backs looking up at the cotton wool clouds, exhausted and loving our happy world.

'What are you doing with my dog?' We look up at the menacing figure, and I instantly name him, Bill Sykes. 'Bloody dog. Been looking everywhere I have.'

Defensively Billy is attempting a 'Your dog? It's my dog!' routine. Timber's eyes are showing too much white, and his shivering shoulders and tail tucked between his legs confirm my worst fears.

'You're dog thieves, you are. Where'd you come from then?'

'Clapham,' says Billy. This bewilders me, because we don't. We live just round the corner.

'Clapham,' noted Bill Sykes. 'That's miles away. Why'd you come all that way here, then? Think yourselves lucky there's not a copper around!'

Brutally tugging at the dog-lead, it was obvious to us how he had ill-treated the now terrified dog.

'Eh, mister,' screams Billy, 'he may be your dog, but that's our collar and dog-lead,' and he chased after the man demanding it's return. Now followed a jumble of simultaneous happenings. Timber's accusing eyes looked 'traitor' at Billy. My heart was thumping in my chest. I saw the man remove his trouser belt, gripping two thick inches of Timber's neck as he unfastened the collar and handed it back to Billy. I watched him hook the belt round Timber's neck, and start tugging again, one hand holding his trousers up. Frantically resisting, claws gouging the grass, Timber's head was shaking from side to side.

I was aware of Billy's hand pulling me towards the perimeter of the park where a tram-car was waiting to pull away, and as we jumped on to the platform my brother was shouting, 'Timber, Timber'. I saw Timber give an almighty jerk and race towards us. After three strides, Bill Sykes was suddenly spread-eagled on the grass, trousers round his ankles. Timber steeple chased on to the platform..Dimly I had noted the tram's destination board was *'Clapham'*, and Billy read my mind as we three climbed the stairs.

'He'll be looking for us all over Clapham. We'll get off at the next stop and go home.'

Timber is now looking contentedly out of the window, as if he were at the pictures again. Tail sweeping on the seat, his eyes were cameras of satisfaction as he viewed Bill Sykes gradually getting smaller in the distance. He turned towards Billy; the long pink tongue licking his face from chin to forehead. Then I didn't see much more because it was my turn. I felt the hot wet tongue sweep sideways across my eyes. That dog loved the salty taste of my tears.

We were on our way *home*.

Fatal Attraction

by

Elisabeth K Cook

He saw a glimmer in the remoteness, like a dew drop casting a spectrum of colour onto an inert wall. Then it was gone. He searched for it; peering deep into the dark, alien distance. He possessed a desire to capture this wondrous beauty, for surely it was a treasure to be placed among the greatest riches ever discovered.

Without warning it appeared once more, glistening in the night. It was then he realised that there was far more to this inspiring wonder than he could ever have envisaged.

Their dark, black, desiring eyes met.

He moved his slender legs, elegantly, gracefully, charmingly, as he courteously performed his courtship dance. Under the intense gaze of the moon, as its beams of light hit his body, he looked like a graceful ballet dancer, expressing his love for a fair maiden through his elegant movements. The moonlight made his movements more fluent and expressive than any tutor could have managed to do.

He was drawn towards her, due to her enticing gestures. It was as if some wondrous force was pulling him to his destiny. He was enchanted; instantaneous ecstasy befell him. She had captured his whole being, he had no control over his weak and feeble body. She had selected her prey and for him there was no escape. Under her power he advanced, a thick sticky substance dripping from his face onto the ground, forming a pool of saliva and slime, as he drooled in anticipation.

With her sleek arms, that felt and had the lustre of silk, she motioned to him to come closer. It was the fulfilment of his every desire. He stumbled nervously, clammy with hot breath that hit her intense face like a scorching arrow. She could feel life being formed within her. There was a creature within her that she had had a part in creating. A sense of horror was growing within her, although her offspring and the source of her power were one. To her, her offspring were a testimony of the power that she possessed. A union had already been formed between her and her offspring. She was isolated from her surroundings and only aware of the tiny beings developing within the pit of her stomach.

All at once she became aware of someone else's presence. The one who was infatuated with her, who would not envisage partaking in the nuptial delights he had just experienced, with any other. She grasped the power she had within her, that which had been revealed to her when she had created a living being. She took hold of that power and manipulated and disfigured it, making it into a power of life and death. Her partner had played his part in this short production and it was now time for him to leave the stage.

She approached, her mouth watering. It was then that he was to discover his true destiny. The thin, watery saliva ran from her mouth as she sank her teeth into his neck. Slowly she began to gnaw at the flesh as her cannibal inclinations were aroused. The bones cracked as she broke them in her teeth, teeth that were like sharp, flashing knifes and just as fatal. The combination of cracking bones being crunched with delight and raw flesh being eaten with vigour provided both sickening sound and horrific views for those passing by.

Soon her feast was over, she had consumed both brittle bones and juicy flesh that had dripped with crimson blood. She turned to her dew-covered web of silk, that sparkled like a diamond in the moonlight, to lay her larvae. The larvae that would do to her as she had done to her mate, once she too had served her purpose.

Administrative Error

by

John Mattocks

Beep ... Beep ... Beep ...
  'Mmmm... What?'
Beep ... Beep ... Beep ...
  'What the hell is that?' he thought.
Beep ... Beep. ... Beep ...
Voices began to drift into his head.
  'He seems to be coming out of it.'
Beep ... Beep ... Beep ...
  'Call Doctor Murray at once.'
The sound of hurrying feet fade into the distance.
Beep ... Beep ... Beep
  Light began to seep into his eyes, hurting, burning into his skull. He was immersed in a cocoon of confusion and helplessness.
  A small green light was bouncing in time to the Beep ... Beep ... Beep...
  'Ah, Mister Craven, you've decided to come back to us then.'
  The voice of a man. Scots, with an air of authority about it.
  'Now don't worry,' he said. 'You will feel a little strange for a while. Mister Craven. Mister Craven!'
  The Doctor turned to the Sister. 'Keep a close eye on him. Let me know when he's a little more lively.'
  He studied the various charts.
  'Yes, everything is looking decidedly optimistic, wouldn't you say Sister. I'm afraid this will take a little time, but he's over the worst now. Good day to you Mister Craven. Good day Sister.'
  Foot steps drifted into the distance again.
  The words, scarcely pierced through the veil of confusion. A thought passed through his muddled brain, 'Mister Craven. Who the hell is Mister Craven?'

  'Jim. Jim. It's me. Jim, please wake up.' A woman's voice. Pleading, anxious.
  He opened his eyes. It was very bright. Night had come and gone.
  'Oh Jim, you've come back to me,' sobbed the woman.

She leaned over and hugged him tightly.

'Oh Jim, I've been so worried. I thought I'd lost you.' She broke down and started to cry uncontrollably.

'Please stop. I... I'm okay. Really,' he said, bewildered. He looked into her tear streaked face. 'Look, I'm very sorry to say this, but I...', he suddenly changed his mind, '... but is there any chance of a drink?'

The worry and strain dissolved from her face, replaced with a huge grin. She dabbed at her eyes as she poured her husband a large glass of orange.

Over the next few days, much was explained to Jim and Hazel Craven about the consequences of falling out of trees, fractured skulls and loss of memory.

Jim had no recollection of anything. Nothing was familiar to him. Not even his own reflection. He hid the full extent of his memory loss from his wife, thinking that she had been through enough at the moment.

He had been in a coma for two weeks and stayed in the hospital another two weeks after regaining consciousness.

He returned home to a house he did not recognise. He was told that he would have to stay home for at least six weeks with regular visits to his doctor. He hoped and prayed that something would start his mind functioning again. Nothing happened for the first two weeks. He was beginning to think that his past had gone forever.

It was morning. Jim lay in bed thinking of his recent experience, trying to recall any fragments of his past. A vivid scene flashed before him. He was suddenly in a familiar room, church bells were ringing.

'Did I used to live here?' he wondered. He moved to the window and saw a huge church with a massive spire. No, it wasn't a church, it was a cathedral. A woman's face appeared before him, pale faced with long, jet black hair. Her eyes were very dark, hypnotic.

The vision dissolved and he was back in his bed. The woman in the vision was as unfamiliar as everything else had become.

He leapt out of bed with a sudden determination.

'I'm going to find that place,' he promised himself.

He studied the road map. He had two local choices; Rochester or Canterbury. Instinct told him Rochester.

He told his wife he was going to have a drive to clear the cobwebs. He didn't want to tell her about the episode earlier that morning. Well, not yet. He hadn't forgotten how to drive. Puzzled, he shrugged his shoulders, and not forgetting the map, he set off for Rochester.

The nearer he got to the city, the more the surroundings became familiar. When the cathedral was in sight, he became excited.

'I know this place. I've been here. At last, somewhere I feel at home,' he said out loud. He parked the car and ran to the cathedral. Standing there, he looked around, intently studying the adjacent buildings. He knew the placed he was looking for was within sight of the cathedral. On the opposite side of the road was the object of his quest. The discovery startled him. A feeling, as if someone had walked over his grave, coursed through his body.

He ran over to the elderly, pale green house, narrowly avoiding another accident, this time with a speeding car.

'Damn! Don't want to end up in hospital again. Just calm down a bit,' he thought to himself.

It was a three storey house that had been divided up into flats. Climbing the steps at the entrance, he examined the names alongside the door bells; *M Hills, John Riley, Mr T S Ashley, P Matthews*. Peter Matthews! The name hit him like a sledgehammer.

His hands were shaking when he rang the bell. He waited. He rang it again, impatient, not really knowing how to handle this situation. What could he say.

He was still contemplating this, when a voice startled him.

'Can I help?' She was a rather attractive girl. Concern showed in her eyes.

'Do you know where Peter Matthews is?' he inquired.

'Oh, you don't know then?' she said. 'Look I think you'd better come in.'

Her name was Michelle Hills. She had to explain to Jim that Peter Matthews had tragically taken his own life after his wife had walked out. She had got to know him just after she moved in two years ago. The grief showed in her face. It was only six weeks ago that the terrible evil thing happened and she had not yet come to terms with the loss. They were very close friends and she felt lost without him. She never really liked Pete's wife. There was always an awkward atmosphere when she was around.

'How did you know Pete?' Michelle asked.

Jim thought about the question, then decided to tell her the truth.

'So you never knew him then? What a strange story. What does it all mean?' she wondered.

'God knows,' thought Jim, shaking his head. 'Thanks for asking me in, I appreciate that,' said Jim. 'I suppose I'd better be going.'

'There is one more thing. On the day it happened, a mystery woman was seen coming down the stairs. Nobody knows who she is. The police tried to trace her but,' she shrugged, 'nothing.'

'Was he having an affair?' he asked.

'Yes he was. His wife found out and she walked straight out, but he wasn't involved with the mystery woman. Well. Not as far as I know.'

He wasn't sure if he wanted to ask the next question.

'What did she look like?'

'Tim Ahsley, he lives in the second to top flat, saw her as he was going in his front door,' she explained. 'He said she was quite stunning. She liked black . Black clothes, black hair. He also mentioned her eyes. Very piercing dark eyes.' A shiver ran up Jim's spine.

'Are you okay?' asked Michelle. 'It looks like you've just seen a ghost!'

When Jim Craven arrived home he was desperately confused. He had been full of hope when he left on his journey. What had started as a quest for enlightenment, some kind of clue to his past, became another muddled enigma. He was beginning to doubt if he'd ever find his past.

So, dear reader, time to explain. Let me introduce myself. I have been called many things in the past; The Grim Reaper, The Bringer of Death, etc. Very grim, gloomy names, I'm sure you'd agree? I'm just doing my job, that's all! Sometimes, though, I do make mistakes. Well, I'm only ... human.

Allow me to explain.

You've all heard that everything in the universe has a purpose. Yes? Well that's not strictly true.

Jim Craven died and he shouldn't have. Administrative error, you see. His soul escaped me, therefore, I needed another one. Simple, isn't it? Peter Matthews was expendable, so my assistant paid him a visit. She told him she was carrying out a market research survey on chocolates. Drugged, of course. Totally painless. He was found hanging from the attic later that day. His soul was collected and sent back down into James Craven's body. You see, James Craven is to father an important child soon, one that will truly benefit the whole world in forty years time. It's such a shame that the real James Craven has gone. Still, Peter Matthews has got a new lease of life.

Dreaming

by

Susan Prescott

Lynda picked up her shopping bags from the check-out counter and wearily trudged to the automatic doors. It had been a miserable morning. Her youngest child Sam had tried to get out of going to school yet again, by complaining of a stomach-ache, although he probably hadn't done his homework or he had got a games lesson. At fourteen he was at that age where all he wanted to do was play on his computer or be out with his friends until all hours, Lynda certainly couldn't get a word out of him these days.

It had been raining when she had got up this morning, Phil, her husband of twenty years mumbled a 'Good Morning' to her as he stumbled out of bed and into the bathroom.

Breakfast, as usual was a hurried affair with everybody getting under each other's feet. Chloe, her daughter of sixteen couldn't, surprise, surprise find her school books, shoes, purse, tie etc. The usual shouting match ensued, with Sam and Chloe fighting over a pen and it all ending with a bowl of cornflakes smashing to the floor.

After finally getting rid of the kids to school and her husband to work, she cleared up the soggy cereal and washed up the remaining breakfast dishes. Then she set off to do her weekly shop.

When Lynda was out of the supermarket, she called for a taxi (just this once). While she was waiting the rain stopped and the sun crept out from behind the clouds and smiled down on her. Back home she proceeded to put her shopping away and then prepared the dinner for the evening. Monday nights was always Shepherd's Pie from the leftovers of the roast from the day before. It seemed to her like a good idea, but of course the kids hated anything that didn't come with chips at their ages.

The sun was really beating down its rays now and Lynda, grateful for an hours peace went into the garden, dragged the old holey deckchair from the shed and sat down.

'I deserve this,' she spoke to herself quietly and she closed her eyes. Not surprisingly she was soon in a deep sleep, completely shut off from everything around her.

First she heard the waves crashing in the distance, then music came to her, it was lively and she wanted to get up and dance all her cares away. Then came the smell of food, a gorgeous smokey aroma was wafting in her direction, maybe a large T-bone steak or a mouth-watering Prawn Kebab. She was trying to imagine what sort of sumptuous cream filled dessert to have when a hand lightly touched her shoulder. She jumped up with a start and found herself staring into the eyes of the most heavenly body she had ever seen. His skin was a rust brown colour, probably from spending a long time on a surf-board, she mused. His hair was shockingly white, bleached by the sun and his eyes were bright blue, they nearly matched the azure of the sea. He spoke softly and enquiringly,

'Would the lady like a Cocktail?'

Lynda gazed into his eyes and he smiled at her, the most delectable smile ever.

'A Pina Colada, I think,' she stammered trying to keep her words controlled and not look out of place. He turned and walked across the sand to the awaiting bartender.

Lynda pulled herself up and gazed at the delightful scene surrounding her. Palm trees, soft golden sands and dolphins dancing in the sea, and not a glimpse of seaweed anywhere. Just where was she?

It was a dream, she knew that, but then it was her dream so she could make anything happen, couldn't she?

She got up from her lounger and started to walk towards the bar. It was a round building, the bottles displayed went all around it and there was probably a kind of beer from every country in the world. The seats around the bar were high backed and sitting on them were men and women with perfect bodies and laughing happy faces. Lynda then looked down at herself, she wore a scarlet high cut bikini and she too looked perfect, her thighs had never been so thin, after all it was her dream.

The music was getting louder with a more definite beat perhaps Jamaican or African. It certainly made Lynda want to dance. The young man with the striking blue eyes was looking at her again. In his hand was the biggest drink she had ever seen in her life. The glass had umbrellas and mixed fruit in it, and even a sparkler fizzing away in it.

'Your Pina Colada madam, with our compliments.'

She looked around and a dozen or so people raised their glasses towards her.

'Thank you,' stammered Lynda, still unsure of herself in these new surroundings. She took a sip and the cool liquid slipped down her throat and made her feel like a young girl again. And then she saw him sitting at the bar. It was Phil, her husband of twenty years, he was drinking from a bottle of beer of some foreign origin. He waved to her and gestured her to go over. As she walked closer she noticed that he was different somehow. He looked leaner, fitter there were no lines around his eyes and his face looked happier not the 'I had a hard day at work' frown it usually bore. Then she realised, it was Phil, but twenty years younger. It was like he hadn't changed from their early courting days.

'I've been waiting, darling,' he said as she reached him. 'Would you like to dance.'

Her heart seemed to glow and a broad smile erupted across her face. She slid into his arms and they danced like they had never danced before. The tempo slowed down and they clung to each other, Lynda silently wished that dreams could come true. The music slowly came to an end and they drew apart and began to walk towards the sea hand-in-hand.

'Don't you wish it could always be like this,' Lynda asked quietly. She turned to Phil, but his image had disappeared from her mind.

Lynda smiled to herself. She could feel her skin getting wet and as she awoke she found herself back in the real world, the sun had gone in and it had begun to rain once more. She rose from her battered and torn deckchair and went back to her kitchen, with her boring Shepherd's Pie. The kids would be screaming through the door soon and Phil would come in moaning about the office.

'Never mind,' she laughed to herself, 'I can always fly back tomorrow.'

Turkey and Biceps

by

Tom Buckland

I didn't believe her of course. I was just starting to peel the potatoes when I heard the car pull up and she entered in a hurry.

'Hard day at the office dear?' I said.

She shook the rain droplets from her umbrella.

'Not bad. And you, how was your day?'

'The same my dearest, housework never gets any easier.'

'Here let me do that,' she said as she took the knife and began peeling the potatoes, 'you always make it look such hard work.'

'I'll make us a cup of tea then,' I said as I tried to hold on to my esteem.

'Oh by the way Mr Schwarzenegger's coming to Christmas dinner,' she said as she lit the stove.

'And is he bringing Madonna with him?' I laughed.

'No just Mr Schwarzenegger. You know, the film star, he played Terminator or something. He came to the office today. Our company handled the public relations for his large contribution to Oxfam. He was so pleased with all the good publicity that he dropped in to say thanks personally.'

'And I suppose he just came up and invited himself to our house for Christmas dinner,' I said trying not to snigger.

'Not quite,' she answered, 'when he walked through the office he stopped and remarked on what lovely legs I've got.'

'I'm always telling you that you wear your skirts too short,' I said truthfully.

This didn't go down too well.

'Don't start, it's the fashion,' she insisted, 'anyway as I was telling you, he told me what lovely legs I've got. I in turn told him what lovely muscles he's got especially his biceps, just to hold them, they're so firm, so... well we talked for a while and I invited him for dinner which he accepted. Won't the neighbours be jealous.'

I still didn't believe her. Arnie Schwarzenegger coming to our humble house. Never.

The weeks went by with nothing more said about it. I put it down to being one of those silly moments that all women seem to have now and again. Then three weeks before Christmas we were shopping in Tescos.

'We had better get the turkey,' she said.

Turkey! It looked more like a jumbo jet.

'What the hell do we need that for?' I said trying to bring her to her senses.

'Mr Schwarzenegger is bound to have a healthy appetite so I want to make sure we've got enough food.'

So it started again. It didn't matter how much I tried to speak sense to her, she still insisted he was coming to dinner.

'What do you think men built like that like to eat?' she asked.

'Men like me,' I nearly replied.

I went and saw our Doctor.

'You must understand she's getting to the age where she could be starting on the change of life. The hormone imbalance creates some physiological problems. I'll pop in when passing by,' he said trying to reassure me.

He did but it never changed things.

She kept on so much that even I started to believe her. One day I told my work mates that the big Hollywood star Arnold Schwarzenegger was coming to see us at Christmas. They never let me forget it.

'Going to show him how to get a body like yours,' they would laugh or,

'The wife wants a real man in her Christmas stocking does she?'

I was glad when the holidays started.

Christmas eve I never saw much of her. Cleaned the house from top to bottom she did. Then did it again.

'Can't let Mr Schwarzenegger see our house untidy can we dear,' she would say as she scampered past with feather duster.

Christmas morning was nice. I bought her an Aran jumper a size too big. She bought me an Aran jumper a size too small. We swapped them, they fitted perfectly. It's little things like that which make Christmas.

We always have our Christmas dinner at exactly two-thirty. Not a moment before nor a minute past. At two o'clock she was standing at the living-room window watching anxiously.

'I hope Mr Schwarzenegger's not late,' she said looking worried.

I wanted to tell her it was nonsensical this charade, but as I was about to speak something caught my eye. A black Limousine pulled up outside our gates. It must have been the length of four cars, out jumped five bodyguards all built like American footballers. Then he got out making them look like school boys in comparison. God he must have been eight foot tall. Well he looked eight feet tall. He clipped a mobile phone to his belt saying something to his bodyguards, they jumped back into the Limousine and drove off. He knocked on the door and she opened it for him.

'Come in Mr Schwarzenegger, dinner's nearly ready.'

He took her hand and gently kissed it.

'And I'm sure it will be a gastronomical delight,' he said.

The afternoon wasn't as bad as I thought it was going to be. He was well spoken, well behaved and interesting company. Then at the end of the meal things started to deteriorate. He took out a Cuban Davidoff cigar.

'I'm sorry Mr Schwarzenegger we don't allow smoking in this house', I said.

He smiled.

'Call me Arnie,' he said as he slapped me on the back nearly putting my dinner straight back on the plate.

He didn't smoke it. He ate it. The wife was suitably impressed. I picked up one of the table candles and bit on that. It didn't have the same effect somehow.

It was a few moments later that my wife was discussing her collection of fine bone china thimbles.

'How interesting,' he said.

'Would you like to see them?' she asked as she rose and walked towards the stairs, 'they're in the bedroom.'

He started to follow her as she walked up the stairs. I tentatively put my hand on his arm.

'You won't do anything will you? With my wife I mean.'

He brushed past my out stretched arm, stopped and looked back at me grinning.

'Trust me,' he said.

Twenty minutes they were up there. Twenty minutes. I mean how long does it take to look at china thimbles. When they came down I'm sure I noticed a glint in his eye. He looked at his watch.

'Hey guys it's been great but time's up. I've gotta go.'

He took his phone said something like come now and within fifteen seconds the large Limousine pulled up outside our gates. He opened the door. That is the last we will see of him I thought.

He turned to face us.

'I'll be back.'

'Oh' I thought! 'I can't wait.'

After he'd gone we didn't say much.

'Nice man' she had said as she started to wash the dishes.

'Nice man! He looked at you like a dog on heat, only trouble is he doesn't look like a dog, more like King Kong.'

Once in bed we settled into our normal routine.

She knits while I sit and wish she didn't. I couldn't hold it in any more I had to ask.

'You didn't... well you know, when you came up with him, you didn't do things together did you?'

She looked at me with those big brown eyes.

'Of course we didn't. Whatever made you think that,' she replied.

'He's good looking, isn't he?'

She looked at me with her sweet smile.

'I can promise you in all our time together I've never been unfaithful to you in body or thought. I love you.'

I started to relax.

'I had to ask, you know, to check. After all he's a big star.'

She put her hand on my bare chest and slowly let it run down my body.

'Those rippling muscles are all very well but if I want someone to pin me to the bed then your the only Terminator I'll accept.'

I felt good again, her hands had done their magic, Arnie had gone hopefully for good.

Not a bad Christmas after all. Only one problem. Mr Schwarzenegger, it turned out, is on a diet. What the earth are we going to do with all that turkey!

Oceans of Guilt

by

C R A Pennington

Crashing colours, whirling in a drone of sonic agony gently smoothed into ecstasy. Dim now, the tones faded and peace gradually returned. Suddenly scattered images of captured light cascaded into scintillating shapes and brilliant piercing colours. The melody of sparkling sound produced cloud-bursts of pleasure as sensory impulses raged through my mind. The sensations gradually formed into coherent order and wove an ultimate picture of light and purity.

Lustrous figures formed spinning patterns of perfection, basking in kaleidoscopic beauty. They became a glittering mosaic of perfect flesh as shrill, emotion-scouring screams piped a song for their dance, a minuet which weaved through snowy mists of throbbing translucent hues.

Now I understood. They were infinite reflections of a single goddess of beauty, basking in the silver light of all the mirrors of the world.

I travelled through the swirling patterns towards the focus of the endlessly spinning maze, heading for the final image of pulsating light. The goddess' creamy porcelain flesh glowed in a celebration of form which radiated a warm lustre of immaculate colour. The petal-like delicacy of her skin, the soft sheen of her limbs, the fierce welcome of her scarlet smile, the burning summons of her violet eyes invited me to dance with her.

So we spun as crystal pipes played fruit-soft chords about us. I marvelled at the radiant perfection of her form, the exquisite fire in her eyes, the warmth and velvet of her hair that glowed with an inner auburn flame. We gyrated in an endless paradise of sound and light and pigment. Balance reeled in an orgy of heady intoxication. And then, as her soft embrace took me to feather pillows and soft beds of anticipation, her smile changed...

It took on the shadow of cruelty and pain, it broadened obscenely and an impossibly long, scarlet tongue unrolled towards my tender throat. My goddesses eyes turned blacker than a hellish soul, no light or hope of life escaped them. Her delicate breasts split open along their mid-line as ribs sprang outward from a twisted torso. Scarlet blood gushed from the hole, drenching me in heavy sticky fluid as my mind filled with the throbbing rush of a single inescapable heartbeat. Her unjointed arms flailed like snakes trying to crush the breath from my body, drawing me closer to the bloodied, toothless, torso-maw.

With sudden terror, I seized her boneless neck in a finger locking stranglehold and fought desperately to escape the horror of a vampirish death embrace. And then the dream abruptly dissolved...

Recovering vision I realised whose throat I gripped. Staring in numb disbelief at the limp form lying beneath me, I mechanically released my fingers one by one and began to sob in fear and grief.

It was only when I heard the soft whistle of breath between the lips of her purple face that I could stop crying and bury my head at her warm and beating breast. I waited for the girl I loved to wake.

From that night onwards there grew an invisible barrier between us. We weren't the same as before, it was as if my dream signalled to her my true feelings. Then one night we rowed and she said she couldn't be with someone who didn't really love her and she left disappearing into the cold of the night, leaving me to fumble over the words which I hadn't said, the three words which she needed to hear as much as I needed to say them. Then something came over me, a wave of realisation. If I had to say the words she wanted to hold on to the thing I cherished most in my life then I would say them, I would say them and break down the wall of doubt between us. I raced out into the dark after her, to the beach where I knew she would be. I ran to tell her that I loved her.

It was as though she stood inside a giant cavern whose walls were made from gloomy, swirling colours which occasionally parted to admit rays of light from the moon. As the moon pierced these walls, stained them grey and black, it was hard to believe that they were merely clouds massed above cliffs and a troubled dark sea.

Thunder rolled in the distance and flickers of light attested to the ferocity of that far off storm. A light rain fell from clouds that were never still. They traced colossal patterns in the sky, like the flowing robes of people performing a purposeful, trance-like dance, moving to the music of the clouds and the rain.

And the sea below seemed weary of the endless motion at its surface. Great waves heaved themselves together then sighed with relief as they crashed against the sharp, ragged rocks of the shore.

She stood gazing out to sea, hair tumbling across a freckled face as the wind tugged at her flapping clothes, unable to penetrate the vaporous perimeter of her present prison. She turned and walked carefully over the stones on the beach, disappearing behind the mist-like spray of a breaker, dashing its brief life against the rugged shore's teeth and yet in so doing, liberating its watery soul to fly upon the breath of the tumultuous heavens.

I watched her move on the rocky beach, wreathed in spray from a dying wave's last roaring cry to the skies. In my mind's eye, I saw a creature which swam slowly through deep, cold waters, a looming shadow, sleek and black, shark-like in its endless circling of an ocean who's water was at one instant crystal clear but at the next became clouded with a million tiny bubbles.

This was also the creature which troubled my dreams and sometimes, in my blackest moods came to the surface to crash through the waves and writhe, unchecked in the swirling foam. It was a shark inhabiting the dimly lit depths of my mind. It had chased me through eternity in a watery prison, through oceans of dreams, hunting me like a predatory, razor-toothed horror called fear.

'I love you!' were the last words I managed to cry out before she became obscured by the fleeing spirits of the sea. For a ponderous instant I thought she had heard my final plea and turned, but no, the wily water wraiths that danced around her shadowed form had woven a pattern of enchantment to confuse my senses. When I looked again she was gone, drifting towards the deep cold heart of the oncoming storm.

So I left her on the beach, left her to her thoughts, and left her to come back to me when she decided, when she was ready to hear the words that for so long I had been trying to bring myself to say out loud. Shrouded in darkness, I waited for her as seconds became minutes and minutes became hours, all to the sound of rolling thunder so near that it seemed to lurk just outside the window. I waited to say the words we both needed to hear.

A telephone call interrupted the symphony of thunder playing to encourage the first grey tendrils of dawn's early light. Shortly afterwards, a haggard, unshaven policeman drew back a cool white sheet to reveal a naked form which he asked if I knew. For an instant a sickly prickle of recognition came over me, and then I realised that I was mistaken. I had to be mistaken.

The face was remarkably similar, but it had a certain blue tinged pallor which separated it from the colour of the face of the girl I had been with only hours before. Also, my love's eyes were not black rimmed and swollen like the eyes of this girl who stared blankly up at me. This corpse was bloated, too, unlike the delicate frame of my love, who's animated body was probably now still walking along the stormy shore, or perhaps swimming in the sea as she liked to do some mornings. No, this pallid, bloodless thing must not, could not be the girl that I loved.

'It's not her.' I said quietly and fled from this dead girl who looked so like, and yet could not be, the person I knew. So I returned home and not finding her there, I walked to the beach, the place where I had seen her last. But the beach held no trace of life, except the motion of the sea endlessly heaving itself together to form the tired waves that crashed against the stones on the shore.

She liked to swim in the morning, water was as natural to her as the breeze is to the butterfly. I imagined her swimming now, hidden from me by the rolling sea, floating on a swell and luxuriating in its refreshing, brisk chill. So, kicking off my boots, I picked my way to the water's edge, ankles wetted by the encroaching wash. If I could find her in the sea, I could prove that she didn't lie on the cold stone slab in the mortuary. Throwing my jacket on to the dew damp stones behind me, I moved forward, wading into the cold, murky water, bracing myself and plunging in to my shoulder, propelling myself with tired arms and legs.

I shouted for my love over the roar of the sea and began my search, knowing that when I found her we could be together forever.

The Wild Goose Chase

by

Neville Taylor

Ali had now been travelling north for three days. He was seeking news of his older brother who had not returned home from a holiday in northern Nepal. His brother, with three climbing companions, set out to trek through the Sagarmatha National Park. They had flown to Luckla, in the Khumbu district. Their plans had then been to walk up the northern section of the Dudh Kosi valley and to enter the park by Mondzo and Tengboch. Their way out was westward to Kodari, and the northern highway. Then by bus back to Delhi. There had been a report in the papers, that a Chinese army border patrol had fired on and killed a trekking party. Nothing more. Ali asked for permission to temporarily leave his employment with the International Bank of India, to search for his brother. He was advised to delay his journey, by his employers and family. His boyish desire for adventure, filled him with impatience. Stories of the courage of others filled his mind. Should he find their bodies, he would be famous, if he brought them out alive, a hero. Newspaper and TV reporters would pay a huge sum of money for his story.

He had arrived in Kathmandu, on the noon bus from Birgunj. Kathmandu, he thought, was a pretty city. A city of two worlds; the haves and the have not. The magnificent palaces and large houses of the very rich, were sheltered from the hovels of the untouchables by a fringe of buildings of descending value. The poor, who lived in the urban area, dwelt by the river. The river provided most of their needs. It sufficed for washing, bathing and it flushed away human as well as, animal waste. It even provided a service to the dead.

He secured a place to sleep at a very cheap hotel, twenty rupees for a space in a dormitory room to lay down his bed roll. Food was not available. Down the street he found an eating house. A bowl of Daal bhat, rice and lentils, was the only item left on the menu. To supplement, there was plenty of fruit to be had, later, to be washed down with a cup of Chang, or tea. When he got back to the dormitory, it was full of smelly snoring bodies.

He was up early next morning, to catch the first bus going north to Kodari. He had no set plan of action, he had never thought of what he was going to do. A boy from the plains, could not envisage the wilderness of the mountains. Kodari, was where his brother had intended to make for, that seemed as good a place as any to start. The bus was crowded, he had found a seat, yet there were as many standing as sitting. The sun's rays were still not on the street, yet so early, it was warm. The air inside the bus was stale, a mixture of unwashed bodies, smoke, beer and discharged human gases, perverted the early morning freshness. To escape this stench, perhaps, once outside the urban area, the driver may permit him to ride on the roof among the baggage. This had been sometimes possible on his journey so far. It all depended on the willingness of the driver and the police. Not all the police along the way had been so tolerant. Outside the built up areas, the rural police were not so strict.

Just before the bus left the Kathmandu valley at Bhaktapu, the bus stopped for a short while for the comfort of the passengers. Here the driver let about ten of them climb onto the roof. The rush of air caused by the forward progress of the bus was cooling, fresh and sweet. There was more to see now, the view here was not so restricted. Sal trees and giant bamboo grass lined the road. The trees provided a canopy to temper the heat of the sun, while the cool green colour of the bamboo, always so beautiful, absorbed the glare, soothing the eyes. The elevation of the road was increasing. Every so often, there were breaks in the forest, which permitted long views into the valley below.

The road was still getting higher and the vegetation shorter. Bamboo, had been left behind, there were still a few Sal trees, the rest, Ali could not name. As the afternoon passed, it got cooler, the sun's rays sank, coldness set in. Sunset in the mountains is an ever changing kaleidoscope of colourful imagery supplemented by a breath taking coloured neon light spectacular. Then quickly darkness falls, like a descending roller blind shutting out the afternoon sun.

The bus reached Kodari, two hours behind darkness. Ali was cold, deep into the bone and all the way down to his feet. He had never experienced cold like this before. The plains of northern India were comparatively hot, even in the winter time. He found a place to stay similar to the one in Kathmandu. He greedily ate his bowl of Daal bhat, savouring the warmth and quickly drank two portions of tea. Immediately afterward he rolled into his bed to get warm and eventually fell asleep. He did not get up quite so early the next morning. He woke early enough, but now he had to think and then plan what he was going to do. The excitement he had felt on leaving Delhi, had now evaporated, a kind of numbness possessed his brain.

When he hit the street the day was getting warm. He did not feel like eating but, he forced himself to drink some hot tea. Kodari, was a one street town.

Just the same as most border posts. All the usual business houses were open, there were no cars in sight, just a few ramshackle vans and lorries. Perhaps the business traffic would come later. Reflecting on yesterday's journey, he could not remember seeing much traffic then either. What sustained this town's existence?

He had agreed with himself, that his first move must be the Police Office. Here, it was at the far end of the town and doubled as the border post. Outside the building, four policemen were sitting on the ground playing a game, which consisted of tossing small stones into a number of cup shaped holes in the ground. When he asked to speak with the one in charge, he was motioned to go round to the back of the building. He found a man sitting under a lean to, made out of a suspended blanket. The policeman was most unhelpful. Yes, he had heard about the shooting. No, he had not seen anyone who had. Perhaps it was all a mistake and there had been no shooting. How long could one survive out there? At this time of year no problem if one had food and water. Was it possible to raise a police search party? Yes, if there was proof that someone was lost. But, in this case, no.

Ali, walked back up the street to the hotel dispirited. He could not think what to do next. He now realised he was a man of the plains, not the mountains. He had a little money with him, but he had arranged, before leaving Delhi, that he would send for more if he was in need. There must be someone in the town to whom he could talk. He went to the cafe and bought some tea. He asked the owner if he knew anyone who could help him? He said the guides, both local and national, congregated at the Bar further along the street. When he had finished his tea he went along there. He soon learned of a number of guides who would undertake to help him for one-hundred rupees a day plus food. Selecting one, he explained his problem to him. The guide said it would be difficult to know where to look. If they had not ventured from the known trails they would have been seen by now by other parties or the nomads. If, on the other hand... there was no telling where they may be. The region out there was vast and bleak. It could take a long time. Disheartened, still further, he resolved to take the bus back to Kathmandu. There he could visit the Nepal branch of the International Bank of India, and arrange the transfer of more money.

When he asked to see the bank manager in Kathmandu, he was told he would need to make an appointment. Two days time was the soonest he could be seen. Explaining to the receptionist the urgency of his case. She said, 'No matter, two days. He could see the chief cashier now, if that would do.'

When he introduced himself to the chief cashier, he said, 'yes, there is a message waiting here for you. Your brother and his friends arrived home the day after you left. They were never lost.'

Rings of Gold

by

Tessa Lawton

Summer is at its height. The fields of golden wheat and corn stand proud; shimmering in their dance as they stretch upwards to the sky. Their time has come and they proudly wait.

The world is waiting; an expectant air falling across it like a mysterious veil. Any day now the machines will move in and execute the beautiful crops. But will it be too soon?

For the time has come for the circles to appear. Those strange shapes that start to form as if by ancient magic crafted. Some perfect in their dimensions. Others criss-crossed by strange lines. All cutting into the landscape and leaving the world wondering. A people without an answer. So now they watch. They watch by day; sitting in the shadows cast by ancient trees. They wait by night; their small fires making a random line of beacons from coast to coast.

Sometimes the watchers stand up. Was that gust of wind some tiny whirlwind that would explain the shapes? Is that hare pursued by a fox running in a perfect circle? And then they sit back down, or perhaps go home, knowing that today brings no answer. Tomorrow is another day. The next village has another field. Perhaps then they will be more lucky.

For some a logical explanation does appear. At night small groups of people arrive, creeping stealthily towards the sleeping field. With great care, their voices hushed to quell their giggles, they creep between the stalks. Not one must be touched until they reach a safe distance. And then they use a rope and transform into a human compass. Their leader in the centre, the followers treading barefoot around and around in a giddy dance. The circle is complete.

On hills shrouded in mysterious legends, the devout stand, binoculars in hand. In the shadows of the night they appear like members of an ancient religious cult. Their warm coats taking the shape of robes. The crucifix metamorphosed into the glasses that bring the heavens closer. They watch the sky for lights, like the star that once appeared to men in the East. But these watchers have no idea who they are waiting for. Or what. The one thing that binds the groups together is that they wait for something - anything - that may lift their life out of the rut. They grow weary of the day to day struggle, and the search diverts them.

But the answer will not come in their lifetime. Those that do hold the answer hold on to its secrets like a precious gift. Something so tender and precious that it cannot be shared.

The ones that seek the truth are not the ones that will ever be enlightened. The change will be slow. Barely perceptible. There will never be any sudden moment of answering.

Through the ages it has always been the same. Those that seek mystery find nothing but dull fact. Those that live a life ruled by the heart have enlightenment thrust upon them.

For my part, I walked alone in the rosy evening light, searching for nothing more than peace. Another day had been spent surrounded by people, yet alone. A misfit of society. No belief to sustain me. No expectation to lift me. Twenty-five years living in a land where I am a stranger. I knew there was much beauty in the world; a great capacity for love within my heart. But no-one could fill the gap.

The evening gave way to night and I turned my back on the horizon. There was hardly a sound left in the world now. Just the cries of an owl and the singing of the corn. It felt wonderful.

And then I knew that somebody was with me. I knew instinctively that it was a man. And I knew that there was no reason to be afraid. The voice of the rustling corn changed, telling me to trust and feel at ease.

My whole being responded, filling me with such warmth that I had never felt before. This was the feeling that had eluded me all through life. I was no longer alone. My time had arrived.

When he appeared I knew that this was the whole purpose of my existence. This one chance meeting. One small moment in time that would fulfil all my wishes and desires. A few hours set in the midst of an existence that would sustain me forever.

I had never dreamt that such eyes could exist. Large, dark and sparkling; speaking more than any words could express. I was drawn to them and then into them. Falling happily into a place of total bliss where two worlds melted into one; two hearts blended.

His skin was pale and perfectly white, covering bone structure that gave him strong features. And his hair was the golden colour of the corn that brought us together. Tousled by the wind into waves like those that rippled across the fields; begging me to touch it.

When his hands reached out for mine, I did not hesitate to join them. At once the thoughts from his mind were linked with mine. I understood everything. Where he had come from. Why he was with me now. What was expected of me. All the thoughts that had puzzled me over the years were explained in one touch.

The answer to the mystery of the circles was handed to me, as it had been to other women. And I knew why our ancestors had laboured to build circles of stone. Why Stonehenge was dragged into place in a desperate attempt to bring them back. Even then it was known that this time would come. But it could not be rushed.

As we made love, I knew that this experience would sustain me for the rest of my life. No human being could match his touch. Never again would I have to wonder exactly what love was. His tenderness was total. We were two halves, forced apart by time and space, but now joined in mind and body.

Words were not necessary. Neither were goodbyes. Just a gentle touching together of heads that ensured we are linked forever.

When two beings are joined in marriage, their symbol is a golden band. A circle of gold. Just as he and I are linked by the marks of the UFO in the bright yellow corn.

And across the world, other women are joined in the same way. We are the only ones who know the secret. And what if we were to speak about it? We would be ridiculed. We would be outcasts. We would be examined. All the beauty would be lost or dirtied.

And our young babies would be taken from us. The children of another race that will, in time, draw us closer to that other world. Each year the population swells in numbers, scattered across the globe. But until they are ready to take over, we must remain silent, giving the children the chance to grow in power.

The take over will not come in the form of a war. It will be a gentle blending of races that will ensure the earth retains its beauty forever.

The golden circles of corn, leading mankind in full circle, returning him to the earthly paradise.

Famous Folk From Bristol

by

Michael Rose

I met an old man the other day whose name was once held in reverence in this town. Younger people may have heard their father mentioning him from time to time, but now he is all but forgotten. So earlier this week I caught up with the former boxer, who is now blind and begs a living, the man's name - Bobby Rose.

I picked Bobby up from his regular Saturday spot where he begged money at the Bristol City Football Ground and drove him back to his house. He lives in a run down part of the city in a cheap bedsit, and like its occupants it has seen better days. It was once an opulent area where all the slave traders had their large mansions with their cast iron balconies over looking the Clifton Bridge and Gorge. Now their great days were over they have all been turned into flats and bedsits by greedy landlords. The roofs have cracked tiles, the parapets are crumbling and they all need a lick of paint but they still put on a facade of grandiose dignity. The houses still peered over the town but now in a more humble manner. As we slowly wound up the twisting roads to the top Bobby nostalgically told me some of the history of the places we had passed. Even though he was blind he still knew by the twists and turns of the car where we were. We walked through a maze of alley ways and passages, and all around the place old men sat resting in the sun and they all shouted out a cheery hallo to Bobby.

As we entered his room I was prepared for the sight of squalor, but was more than surprised at how tidy it was. Bobby was obviously quite proud of his room and his former military career reflected in it. As he told me, 'A place for everything and everything in its place', would greatly ease the life of a blind man. Apparently a woman neighbour came in once a week to do the more difficult tasks, but where he could he preferred to manage on his own.

He then told me his story. From his very early days at youth clubs and boxing clubs he was handy with his fists so on entering the army Bobby was immediately put down as a boxer. The more he fought and won the more his popularity gathered momentum. So every night he fought there were bigger crowds spurring him on and he grew to love their applause and adulation. For quite a while Bobby reigned at the Labour Club, beating all his opponents.

When the day came that he was told he would be fighting Edward Black, Bobby felt a mixture of apprehension and elation. This fight would either have brought about his downfall or, had he have won, it would have set him up on an even higher pedestal.

From the start of the short fight he knew that it would be different. Eddy was not like the other opponents, he was better. Eddy could sense Bobby's disquiet and used it to his advantage and soon Bobby was floundering under a rain of blows.

When Bobby's eyes were ripped open, at first he was unsure whether he was blind or just could not see because of the blood in them and by then his face was covered in many towels; so he jumped the ropes so as not to appear put down and bravely waved at the cheering crowd. He was then led away for the last time from the ring that had been his for many years.

Bobby went quiet for a while as his memories flooded back to that fateful day. I asked him whether if he could have his days over again he would change anything. He gave me a wry smile and said, 'But I can't can I.'

As I took a final look around his room before leaving I noticed a small pile of pamphlets which stood out, as the room was not surprisingly devoid of books. I picked them up and noticed they were programmes from the times when Bobby was 'Top of the bill'. They were very dog-eared and were probably a last link to his former glory days. I glanced out of the window and the view was magnificent; the deep gorge cutting a scar into the heart of the surrounding hills - just as Eddys' final punch had cut a scar into Bobby's heart. I then left him with his thoughts as his unseeing eyes followed me to door.

Later, I found myself wandering around the back streets musing over what I had learnt about Bobby. I decided to head for a nearby pub where I could sit in silence and ponder about the strong image of the boxer's fractured life. I mentioned my thoughts to the barman who indicated a quite, middle aged man with a sallow, unhappy face slouched in the corner; 'That chap knows something about Bobby for he mentioned him only the other day.'

I went over and introduced myself and explained about my visit to Bobby and wondered if he could tell me anything from an outsiders point of view. The story he told me was so poignant that I have reproduced it exactly as he told it.

'My friends and I often spent our Saturday nights at the Labour Club to watch the boxing. It would cost us threepence to get in and we would get the most out of it by watching everything from the minor bouts to the big fights. For us it was the highlight of the week, somewhere where we could congregate and irritate our elders, spitting and swearing. Then we would argue about the boxers, each of us putting forward our reasons for liking a certain individual as if we were experts on boxing. This in itself would lead to minor skirmishes with the rest of the crowd shouting encouragement.

'All of us admired Bobby he was everything we wished we were, brave, courageous and dignified. I remember the day our dreams came crashing down around us. The fight was tipped as the Big One and we had heard of Edward Black's strength and skill. We stood shuffling around on the sawdust floor waiting for the fight trying to feel aloof and putting on an aura of maturity which was wasted on the crowd as they looked at us in our shorts.

'The room went quiet as the opening ceremonies were gone through. You could feel the tense atmosphere, the room was full of smoke, sweat and anticipation. When the opening bell went the whole room erupted into a wall of noise, my friends and I were screaming quite childishly, as if by shouting the loudest we could help Bobby win the fight. In comparison Eddy's supporters were quite reserved, throwing in useful comments such as 'In with your left' and 'Block with your right'. He was obviously a more capable boxer. Suddenly Bobby seemed to falter, and at once his adversary leapt in with a barrage of blows to his head. Even now as I recall it, it seemed to happen in slow motion, one minute Bobby was holding his own, the next the place was coated in blood. I remember it now as the crimson flowers of blood strew the canvas floor, echoing the colour of his name. One of our members was sick and so we all berated him, but as I stood there trying to give off an impression of indifference I knew in my own mind it was a feeling of revulsion.

'The crowd who had seemed to be holding their breath all started breathing again as of one accord. They knew it was over for Bobby in more ways than one. Now as I look back I realize I had betrayed Bobby by paying to see him fight, by supporting him, by building him up to such a height that the only place to go was down.

'I had all but forgotten Bobby Rose until the other day I had seen him begging at the football ground. I reached into my pocket to throw him all my loose change which was, hauntingly, threepence. It did nothing to alleviate the guilt.'

This chap taught me a lot just as Bobby Rose had taught him. Do I want to be famous?

The Retreat

by

Joan Mitchell

There was a piece of wasteland at the bottom of Bert's garden. Bert had access to it through a wooden door in his fence. When Meg couldn't find him, that's where he had retreated to. They had been married for almost thirty-five years and Bert often wondered why they were still together. Meg was houseproud, Meg nagged, oh how she nagged.

'Wipe your feet. Don't put that there. Where are you going? Don't sit like that. Pick up that newspaper', and so on. Bert would often disappear to the wasteland into the old brick shed.

It was quite a sizeable building, Bert had added a few home comforts over the years. An old garden chair, Meg wondered where it had gone, a little primus, a tin mug, an old cupboard and a backless chair. It was cosy, and as far as Bert knew no-one ever came there.

However he was wrong. Ben and his friend often popped over the fence from next door, climbing the apple tree with the overhanging branch and dropping down. It was their camp, sometimes a robber's den or a space ship. They always left everything as they found it.

Another person discovered the old shed, Sandra an attractive seventeen year old from the village, when walking home one sultry June day was caught in a sudden downpour, without a coat. She spotted a roof over the hedge, found a gap and squeezed through. The shed was a welcome shelter from the torrential rain. As Sandra looked around, her bedraggled hair dripping down her face, she smiled a secret smile. She had thought of a purpose for the old shed. Sandra had many boy friends. There was an army camp a couple of miles from the village, consequently Sandra was provided with a steady supply of admirers. The lads in question soon moved on so Sandra's boy friends were many.

'This,' thought Sandra 'was a good quiet spot to entertain them.'

Other creatures made the old shed a temporary shelter. One year a robin built its nest on top of the old cupboard, only Bert noticed the bright eyes peering at him. The tabby tom-cat from across the way, roved around occasionally, Bert sometimes saw him but the cat never appeared when Ben was in residence. Sandra wouldn't have noticed him anyway, she had other things on her mind.

One night an old tramp moved in. He hadn't walked that way before. The old shed provided a temporary home for a couple of chilly weeks. Bert was confined to the house with flu, and suffering greatly, not so much from the effects of flu but of Meg's constant nagging.

'As soon as I am well enough I know where I'm going,' pondered Bert gloomily. When he did gather strength to venture further afield he found someone had invaded his territory. He soon had it spick and span again.

Meg never knew where he disappeared to. She was only too glad to get him out from under her feet. Bert had secretly purchased a personal stereo. He kept it in the old cupboard, padlocked since the event of the tramp. It also held books, and countless old railway magazines. In his younger days Bert travelled on the railways. He also secretly did the football pools. He wouldn't have been able to under Meg's eagle eye.

The summer holidays came. Ben and Mark spent most of their time in 'their playhouse'. Curiously their visits never coincided with Berts. Sandra visited after dark anyway.

Bert had an awful summer. Meg wanted the sitting room decorated, then the best bedroom. She moaned about the state of the kitchen but for once Bert put his foot down. Meg made him take her to Scarborough for a whole miserable week.

Back home again Meg invited her sister and her husband to stay. Bert disliked his brother-in-law intensely. He disliked his sister-in-law even more. She fussed him. He tried to escape once but she followed him down the garden.

Sandra had taken four different boy friends to the shed, although she preferred a walk across the fields, to the woods in the summer.

The leaves were turning colour when Meg decided to look for Bert during one of his mysterious absences. He had been absent for about a quarter of an hour when Meg donned her stout walking shoes, carefully folding her apron, she put it in the drawer. She wrapped herself in a thick woolly cardigan and methodically locked the back door. Trudging down the garden she passed the tool shed which housed the lawn mower.

'He should be cutting the grass instead of vanishing off somewhere,' Meg thought. On she walked tut-tutting as she veered off the path to avoid a loaded wheelbarrow.

'That should be emptied,' Meg felt herself getting angry.

Bert meanwhile was having a confrontation with a certain young lady. He'd been checking his football coupon, when Sandra, unaccompanied for once, burst in. It was hard to see who was the most astonished. Bert was the first to recover.

'What the hell are you doing here?' he asked. Bert was not unaware of her reputation.

'Sorry Grandad,' Sandra recovered her composure. 'I didn't know it was your place.'

'It's not,' muttered Bert, 'I just come here.'

'So long Grandad see you around.' Sandra was gone.

'Bert where are you?' Meg's voice broke the silence. Bert rose from his chair and made his way into his own garden, there to face his wife's fury bravely.

'Where have you been, all these jobs to be done, it's a disgrace, rubbish - clearing - grass - state - rain - tomorrow then you won't be able to cut it.' Oh she nagged.

It was Ben who found the body in the old shed, three weeks later.

Bert confessed. To escape from Meg's nagging, some said. Many said, Sandra got what she deserved. Meg pursed her lips and said nothing. Somewhere - someone got away with murder.

The Story of How Hannah Lost Her Blues

by

Gavin Wright

Once upon a time, there was a pretty little girl, whose name was Hannah. And one day, when Hannah was walking home from school, she tripped over an orange.

Well, Hannah wasn't just pretty, she was intelligent too, so the first thing she noticed about the orange was that it shouldn't have been blue.

Deciding to keep the blue orange, it being such a unique fruit, Hannah dropped it into her pocket and started skipping. And as she continued on her way, she realised that instead of calling the orange an orange (which it wasn't), she would have to call it a blue (which it was).

The only time that Hannah stopped skipping was when she tripped over the second blue orange. Hannah was a bit embarrassed about making the same mistake twice, but luckily there was no-one around to see her make it, and anyway, now she had two blues, which pleased her.

Hannah walked the rest of the way home, being very careful not to trip over. And when she showed the blues to her family, they were amazed. And from that day on, Hannah carried her blues everywhere she went, and showed them to everyone she met, who were amazed, and she even used them once as tennis balls.

Then one day, a friend of Hannah's who was a little boy, asked Hannah if he could borrow the blues, just for a couple of days. Well, Hannah wasn't just pretty and intelligent, she was nice too, so she said yes.

That evening, the boy, being of mischievous nature, painted the blues with orange paint and the next day he gave them to Hannah, saying they were a gift.

Well, Hannah wasn't just pretty, intelligent and nice, she was generous too, so she gave one of the oranges back to the little boy so they could have one each. And they sat in the sunshine and ate them.

When they had finished eating, the little boy started laughing. Hannah asked him what was so funny, so he told her how the oranges had really been her blues, painted orange, and now they'd eaten them.

Hannah might easily have gotten angry with her mischievous friend but she didn't, and soon she too was laughing heartily.

So Hannah and her friend ran laughing all the way home, and neither of them tripped over any fruit.

King Corn

by

Michael J Hills

Having taken recently a short break in Suffolk, I was returning home on lanes and bye ways to see more of the countryside. The corn fields I had seen shimmering in the heat of the autumn sun now lay cut, their harvest of golden seed all collected, only leaving the corn stalks to be baled when dried by the sun. The thoughts on my way up country of the golden corn swaying in the wind returned to me. It seemed to be saying, 'I am the real saviour of mankind. I am surely King Corn.'

With this in my mind and evening drawing in, it was time to stop for food and local ale. On entering a small but friendly looking inn, my mind still full of joyous thoughts, I ordered ale and turned to the only other man therein. By his dusty clothes it was plain to see he had not long left the fields where combining he had been.

'A good job you are doing. It must be very satisfying to get a good crop of corn,' I said to him.

His reply took me aback somewhat. It was, 'Do you think so?'

Though taken aback, I thought I would try one more tack. 'This year's harvest, by what I have seen, will feed us all and leave some for those less fortunate overseas,' I said to him. His reply was just the same. I had by now taken the bit between my teeth. This man will tell me what's biting him.

'Elaborate on that my man.' Was my rather haughty reply.

'If I must.' He said. 'The bumper harvest that you see will go into storage and be left to rot, unless the men in Brussels can find a better way of destroying it.' He paused for a moment and then added, 'It will also be sprayed with dye so it is unfit to eat.'

I asked, 'But why?'

His reply was, 'To keep the price up and to turn the golden corn you have seen into a colder, harder gold. Now do you see?' were the last words he addressed to me. His eyes turned away. I was glad of that, for tears had welled up inside of me, tears of anger for the greedy men, tears of sorrow for the hungry children, tears of self pity for myself on being so inadequate and not able to change the way of the world.

Haestens's People

by

Paul Swaffer

'Haesten came with eighty ships into the Thames mouth and wrought him a work at Middleton.'
Anglo/Saxon Chronicle AD 893

The Man stood statuesque upon the broken quayside of the old Creek, his shoulder length hair with its first strands of grey flailing against his face; caught and sent by the bitter wind blowing across the narrow water. Small wading birds picked and probed their course across banks of exposed mud in search of food; Oystercatchers all brilliant orange bill and watchful eye, smaller Dunlin scuttling amongst the sunken decaying remains of the old Thames Sailing Barges which had once ruled proudly.

This day and this place was a beacon to the Man; he had felt its pulse deep within his soul for months, even years. Now as he scanned the loneliness of salty openness and ruin, he sensed that he had trod here before, that a part of him had always trod here. Suddenly his whole life was blowing before him in the wind; cold and empty, just as ruined and unmarked as the graves of the old Barges.

And yet, between the certain pulses, the Man still stirred with slight unease. In spite of all, he could not lose the blade of self consciousness which searched beneath his outward, calm despair. All his life the Man had struggled with this fear of challenge to his existence, of exposure to the World of what he felt he really was. He had learnt to disguise the challenge, to reduce it to more subtle constraints upon his living. But deep down, deep and far away from the conscious knowing world, the struggle had destroyed him.

A Gull called hauntingly above the Man's head, breaking through his pensive introspection. On the far bank over to his right, the ancient grappled with the new. Castle Rough, an echoed imprint on the tussocked grass of the Kemsley Downs. The Earthwork fortress of the Danish Northmen, who, led by the Viking Haesten; came twelve hundred years ago to burn then royal Milton, and attempt the conquest of King Alfred's Kingdom.

Poised in strength behind this work of ghosts, the Paper Mill; belching its wasted breath into the ashen sky. The Danes lost their bid for Alfred's land; but the Paper Industry harnessing the water of the Creek for its thirst, chaining the People onto the grinding wheel of the new age; slowly robbed the water of its strength and purity until its foe was done, its War was won. Tasting the poison in his blood, the Man flinched. Reflecting upon the extent of what his race had bartered for the prize of material peace, he felt tired and disabled.

The pulsing was stronger for the Man now. Its resonance filled his soul like a brimming cup, upon which he felt compelled to focus for fear it might spill from him. Away at the Creek mouth, past the Saltings, a mist was forming up, rapid and incongruous with the wind lashed day. The Man screwed up his eyes at its approach, puzzled and yet once strange in h is certainty. The Waders could sense it now, grew anxious and calling. They rose in flight, flashes of black and white life in the expectant air to flee its advance.

Now there were others on the strewn Wharfs. Silent people, drawn forlorn like himself to this day and place. They seemed translucent in their existence to the Man, separate to him in their longing. Only when he met and held their eyes could he comprehend their common purpose. And then, suddenly he knew and understood.

He found himself scrambling across the shoreline of decayed weed and broken shards of Victorian refuse. The others were following as the mist rolled in, its outriders already eclipsing the now muted Mill. Knee deep in the sucking mud and chill water, the Man felt himself briefly Charon, straddling the Styx with his deep purpose. At his back were the other people, all intent on clutching the seed from their spiritual deaths in re-born hope. And he Charon, leading them on.

Out of the mist rose the shape of the boat, its Dragon head lifted back in desperate impulse. It's curled lips taut in the clench of hidden doubt. And at the prow stood Haesten, his helm throwing back the glancing rays of the weak and bitter Sun. He had returned with his army for one last war upon the land, for one last throw of the dice before all that he had breathed for dissolved for eternity into dead archaeology. The Man stood poised in the water with the other silent ones. He felt sure and alive, as one with those around him, and everyone at once; everyone that he had ever known or was to meet. Was this how living used to feel? he wondered.

Towering above them now, the Viking Lord smiled grimly to himself. Then, leaning over the side of the boat; he extended a mailed hand to reclaim the first of his people.

A Handsome Stranger

by

Mavis Foreman

Fifteen years ago Della, a beautiful blonde, had captivated her boss, Edward Stilton; so much so, that he had left his wife and later married her. At first Della had thrived on the attention and money of the much older man, but now, at sixty-five, he was about to retire and she was dreading having him around.

Della was forty-two now. Her hair, with a little help, was as blonde as ever and her figure still merited a wolf whistle. She had had a good time on Edward's money with her fast friends, but soon he would be there every day checking up on her. She shuddered at the prospect and this feeling of approaching imprisonment was enhanced by the sudden appearance of a handsome stranger.

She first saw him in a local cafe while she was having tea with Babs, who lived close by and had been dropping in unannounced for years. He was sitting at a table by the window. Their eyes met and a whimsical, suggestive, little smile played about his lips. It actually made Della blush.

Babs followed her gaze.

'He's interested in you', she said.

'Don't be silly', said Della, but she was pleased.

The next time she saw him she was walking the dog in a nearby park and he was sitting on a bench. She recognised him immediately and sat down beside him. Together they watched her little cairn nosing around the trees.

'Weren't you in the Dutch Tea Rooms the other day?' he said.

He was attractive all right, she thought, younger than her, dark haired with a swarthy complexion. She was surprised she'd never noticed him before and wondered why.

'I've a few days holiday,' he said, answering her unspoken question. 'I'm staying in Maple Road.'

'That's where I live,' said Della.

'I know. In that big, white house.' Della stiffened, but the man smiled disarmingly. 'I couldn't help noticing you,' he said. 'That your father who drives off in that big car every morning?'

She was flattered. 'That's my husband,' she said, and sighed. 'He's retiring soon and I'm not looking forward to it.'

'Hm. You're much younger than him, aren't you?'

'Yes,' said Della, staring into the distance. The man moved closer on the bench.

'What's your name?' he said.

'Della.' She stood up and called the cairn to her.

'I'm Ray.' He jumped up too. 'Hope to see you again.'

Della watched him stroll slowly away and admired the swing of his hips. He was something special and staying just down the road. In fact, she could see the driveway of the rather seedy block of flats from her bedroom window.

The next morning Della was up early staring out and there he was cleaning a battered looking car. It was a warm day and he had discarded his shirt. It was quite a sight.

'What are you looking at so intently?' Edward had come up behind her. She turned with a jump and he put his arms about her drawing her close. 'In a few days I'll be free to be with you all the time,' he said.

'A few days!'

'I'm retiring on Friday.'

Della's heart sank as she pushed him away. 'I hadn't realised it was that soon,' she said, wondering again how on earth she was going to cope.

'We've had our ups and downs,' Edward said slowly, 'but this could be the start of a new and exciting chapter.'

'Oh, Edward,' said Della angrily, 'don't be so ridiculous.' A new and exciting chapter at his age, she thought.

Later that morning Babs called and Della made coffee.

'Edward's retiring this Friday,' she said gloomily, 'and - '

'And what?' said Babs.

'You know that man in the cafe?'

'The good looking one who was eyeing you up and down?'

Della nodded. 'He's staying down the road in those run down flats.'

Babs gasped. 'So you've seen him again?'

'I met him in the park. His name's Ray.'

'And you fancy him? Poor, old Edward.'

Della let out a loud sigh. 'Poor, old me,' she said. 'It's going to be so boring with Edward here all the time.'

'You're lucky you've still got a husband,' said Babs, 'and a rich one at that.'
Della sniffed. Babs could be insufferably pompous, she thought.
That afternoon she set off again for the park, this time without the dog, but there was no sign of Ray and she was surprised how disappointed she felt. Then, as she was on her way home, she saw him walking towards her.
'Hello,' he said, 'fancy a short drive?'
Della hesitated. What did she really know about him?
'Edward will be home soon. I can't linger now,' she said.
'Why did you marry him?'
Della flushed. 'That's an impertinent question.'
'Sorry, but I really want to know.'
'For his money, of course,' Della said boldly. 'I hadn't any of my own.'
'You never really cared for him, then?'
'Not really. Look, I must get back.'
Ray grimaced. 'You're so attractive,' he said. 'Can't we spend a few hours together?'
Della moved closer. 'We might arrange it,' she said.
His smile deepened. 'Meet me here tomorrow afternoon about three. We'll go somewhere in the car. All right?'
Della didn't answer but they both knew she would be there.
The following morning Edward said, 'My last day. There's some farewell drinks tonight - wishing me luck and all that - so I'll probably be late.'
'Don't worry about it,' Della said quickly.
That afternoon she took great care with her appearance before setting off for her rendezvous with Ray. When she reached the flats she noticed that the car had gone, but perhaps he was getting petrol, she thought.
She sat on a low wall opposite and waited. The minutes ticked by and gradually anticipation turned to rage. Finally, at four fifteen, she stomped back home. He had seemed so keen. She couldn't understand what had gone wrong.
With a strange feeling of impending catastrophe, she flung open the front door. There was a white envelope on the mat. It must be from him, and yet? Snatching it up she slit the envelope and sank onto a chair. The writing was in Edward's hand:
'Della,' it said, 'Sadly, the private detective I employed has confirmed all my fears and I no longer intend to spend my remaining years with you. Babs and I are going abroad and I am now looking forward to my retirement. My solicitor will be in touch. Edward.'

Compulsions

by

Sean R Carter

I awoke on the morning of the trial to find the panic already setting in. I felt like I had a fever. My forehead was beaded with sweat and my temperature must have been up several degrees on the norm. And this with the bedroom window open wide, the curtains doing a flailing dance in the gusts, sending the flowery pattern into an ecstasy of coloured rain. These short gusts can't have been travelling at less than thirty miles per hour.

My mind was racing already. I couldn't move; my brain was hogging all the available energy for its own senseless witterings. I noticed for the millionth time - at least - that the crack on the ceiling was growing: was it going along the joists or across them? Was the crack superficial? Or perhaps it travelled right through the fabric of the house. Up through the roof. Perhaps it was a symptom of a fault in the very stuff of the universe. What might come rushing through if it weren't mended soon? I would have to see to it. It shouldn't take too long.

I would do it after the trial. After the trial! I tugged the bed clothes so hard that my knuckles turned white in their distress, and then the sheet tore with a terrible rending sound which knocked my mind out of gear for sufficient time for me to be able to hop out of bed, accomplishing the deed in one movement.

The bedroom door provided only a minor obstacle as I wondered at its simple ingenuity and craftsmanship. It wasn't a door of any particularly special character, but it always closed with a pleasing thud and click. It was a door I couldn't help admiring. And the paint on it! It was so hard. But, of course, under the thick hard paint there was a thin feeble slice of wood entombed forever. A piece of organic material that would never again see the light of day. Not any part of it. I searched it again all over, to discover whether there really was any let up. On top of the door, on the bottom of the door, behind the hinges. This paint was inexorable, it allowed no way out, no hope at all. This wood we would never again witness.

The door handle however I didn't like. It was loose fitting and trembled nervously in my right hand. As I turned it I had the feeling that it was going to leap out of my hand, drop to the carpet and hurl itself at my ankles, gnashing furiously like a crazed rabbit.

The door opened of course and I stood in the frame as I felt the different smells of the house swimming around my nostrils, reminding me of its reality. I shuddered though as I realised that the smells were particles of the objects they smelled of. I vowed to hold my nostrils closed whenever I went near anything unpleasant, like a butchers shop, or a piece of animal detritus. The thought of such an article releasing bits of itself like baby spiders to flow away on the rising air and being inhaled by me made my stomach churn.

In the bathroom I filled the basin and plunged my face below the surface of the water. I opened my eyes and was confronted by the plug and chain. The plug was horribly scratched and all the minute gashes were filled with a white substance, the deposits from all my past ablutions. Even now they were dissolving in the water, penetrating my skin and my eyes.

All this time I wasn't thinking of the trial.

The soap was soft and white underneath, even though the rest of it was pink. I imagined taking a bite out of it, being able to savour the taste, gobbling it all down and feeling satisfied. But then I imagined screaming in pain as forty thousand bubbles ripped their way through my inner ear. I started beating my hips and hands against the wash-basin to rid myself of the thought. I knocked my head against the mirror. I suddenly felt the need to be able to control my thoughts, and I started whistling.

And whistling. I should have known, once I started whistling it was difficult to stop; but once the idea came into my head I couldn't help it. I tried whistling louder, harder, to whistle the compulsion away. But the notes of Midnight in Moscow became harsh and interspersed with rushes of damp air. The melody repeated itself over and over again, and I watched my contorted face struggle with itself in the mirror. I remembered how if you blew air up from your chest it was warm, but when you whistle the air only comes from inside your mouth and doesn't steam up the mirror.

Sitting in the back of the car they brought round for me I watched everyone on the street on either side. The traffic was slow since it was eight-sixteen am, so I had plenty of opportunity to observe. It was marvellous how everyone looked so relaxed. I wondered if their lives were plagued too, but secretly. I drew on my cigarette and thought of trying to push it out of the window without first winding the window down. I imagined ramming the cigarette end against the glass, it bending and burning my fingers, and finally breaking the glass, ripping my arm on the jagged edges and being rushed to hospital only to be found to be dead on arrival. Death by misadventure. Slashed his wrists while trying to throw a cigarette out of the window when it wasn't wound down. I felt my body start to rock as the need to bang my head on the ceiling started to surface.

I opened my window and benzine fumes from the exhaust of the car in front flooded in. I knew this was carcinogenic and so I quickly shut it again. But it was too late, the malignant cells were already starting to proliferate in my body. I could feel them popping into life. The feeling made me break wind. I started thumping my belly, where I thought the cancers were, hoping to bruise the cells and make them die. They were like small apples; one knock and surely they would be bruised beyond recognition. Then they would be cast out of my body. They would be secreted through the pores in my skin, from where they would drop to the ground. I would scatter them wherever I walked, dropping cells like invisible snow. Maybe some of them would grow, sprout into seedlings and develop into a new species of plant?

Sometimes I feel like I could scream and scream and go on screaming forever.

Once, I remember, I saw a man talking to his reflection in a shop window. I knew I wouldn't be able to stop myself beating him, hitting his head with my bare hands, and throw him to the ground where I could direct my flailing kicking feet in his direction. And then I had an urge to beat myself. To bang my fists against my face, to fall to the ground and strike the paving stones with my hands, trying somehow to knock the earth out of its orbit. If only I could push it just so far so it would give up its ghost to the sun.

But it wasn't to be. I saw the dead man and he had blood on his face and I felt like licking it off him, make him clean and presentable for when they came for him.

That was the last time I let it get the better of me to such an extent. I promised myself self-control. It was just a matter of concentrating, or being able to think of something else quickly enough. Maybe. I think about it every morning when, trying to brush my teeth, I attempt to screw the toothbrush into the wall, or when I throw pot-plants out of the window, or whatever.

The Shelves Lay Bare

by

Eileen Ramm

Margaret relaxed. She'd got her two kids off to school, the washing up was done, the beds made, even the dog's bowl scrubbed out for later on, and it was only nine-fifteen am - she was *that* organised this morning. And with thirty pounds in her purse, *and* the right change for the parking ticket machine, she was off to town. She backed the car out of the garage, carefully, as it was a tight fit. There was a definite gleam in her eyes, missing normally, and her whole countenance reeked of anticipation - a rare event. She even waved to the milkman, who never bothered to wave back, thinking she must have meant it for someone else.

It was just three miles to town, not a bad trip, traffic easing off now the kids were at school and the office workers had started. Funny, but she never noticed herself driving or changing gears, or even stopping for the lights on these little shopping trips. Everything seemed to happen automatically, without effort on her part. She generally came back to reality, from wherever she was she could not say, when she laid the car to rest in the car park.

She was glad it wasn't a food shopping trip. She wouldn't have been *that* excited about food. Anyway, she normally reserved the food shopping for Friday morning, when her three-year-old was with her - some sort of mad entertainment for the little one, barging into the backs of other people's legs with her trolley, stopping to throw the odd article in the trolley that generally Margaret managed to put back on a different shelf a few minutes later. Every now and then something strange got through, although it was generally a sponge, her favourite article, she could not resist a coloured sponge, that little one. Well, they were well off for sponges, that was for sure. But it wasn't food she was after today, although she might have to get a few apples and a loaf, she thought, annoyingly. If asked, she couldn't have said exactly what she had come to town for, although Margaret was not the type to browse or go in 'just for a look around'. On the other hand, she didn't have a list, either. She knew she had to *buy*, intended to *buy* would *buy*. The money would be spent by the time her two and a half hours were up, nearly every penny, that she was sure of. After all, she did have two children, a dog and a husband, and she could never say they had all they needed, even at their modest standard of living - there was always something *to buy*.

She knew she wouldn't be going into the big department stores, either. Well, at least not straight off. After all, with thirty pounds to spend, just one item there could easy take all she had with her, and then where would she be? No, she would start off at the chemist. Oh, not to buy tablets or anything at all medicinal. She just liked the sights and smells in there, the little bitsy things on the revolving shelves, and they were cheap, too. She might find it there. She might find *something* there. But what was it she was really looking for this morning? It's not that she'd forgotten - she'd never really known in the first place, yet it was there, somewhere here in town, calling out for her, beckoning her, and she would find it, somehow.

Ah, here's the Chemist. They've put up a new display - Vitamin C blasted all over the place, well it brightened up the shop no end, and it led her to one of her favourite corners of the shop. She picked up one or two jars of hand cream, put them down, maybe it was hair conditioner she was after? Or toothpaste? Yes, we could do with some toothpaste - trouble is, with four people in the house they each would prefer a different one, so who to please? None of them, she decided. We'll have this one here that no one really likes, then there will be no argument over favouritism. And then maybe just one or two of these pretty hair-clips for the girl. Yes, that's nice. Not too much money spent. Plenty of time for that other item, plenty of money too. Let's go across the street to Woolworths - I might find it there. It's bound to be there. They have *most* things there.

Plastic containers. Don't they smell nice, en masse? That's the trouble with these places. They put fifty of the same things together, and its impressive. It's larger than life. It possesses a certain power. Yet you *can buy* just one. And you take it home and it is like a grain of sand sitting there, insignificant, a waste of money, you end up putting it in the back cupboard to gather dust. No, she wouldn't be caught out that way this morning. Besides, there was that other thing she was looking for - she had to find it. But it wasn't here, not in plastics. Maybe in plants? But no. They all looked like they needed a good water, like the price would be reduced any minute, and if she waited long enough she might get a real bargain. But it wasn't bargains she was after this morning, either. Maybe it's in electricals. Better take a trip down electricals. Yes, there was that C battery she needed, and a double plug. A bit expensive, as things go, but never mind, they were both necessary, and still left her with most of the money. Better watch it, though. Better have enough left over. Whatever it was she had really come out for might cost a bit. And she couldn't return without it.

What's the time now? Quarter to eleven. Just another hour left to find it! She would have to leave in an hour to pick up the little one from play-school. Much as she wanted *it*, the little one came first. The children always came first. But why did they, always? When was it that she, who had once come first, became last? There must have been a time when they didn't come first, when she was number one, before they had existed, but that memory was lost in a great grey haze of so many years that it was not real anymore. She supposed there was a time when she considered dealing with dirty socks and cleaning the loo both disgusting and beneath her. A time when she had shopped for clothes that she liked, and bought without worrying about the effect on the bank balance. She had bought one dress with one particular night out in mind, not one dress for the season that might also do the next couple of years, something pretty mundane, 'basic' they called it, something that was hard to date. And the nights out, at least once a week with her pack of friends - the laughter, the interest in her and her job and her triumphs or failures with the men in her life. All *that* was not supposed to matter anymore, was supposed to have been replaced by the joys of motherhood - but was it? She felt mature enough, quite content most of the time, but then an odd kind of feeling would overcome her on certain days, certain mornings, like this.

A sudden jolt in the back from a loaded shopping basket brought her back to reality. Just look at the time! The realities of life began to bear down on her. She had wasted too much time in Woolies. And it definitely wasn't there - she knew it, could sense it. Never had been. Better go around the corner to that department store. Start off in haberdashery, there was always lots of really useful items to explore there. Mind, I don't want to find myself drifting towards the pattern books, something I am prone to do, but this morning there was no time for this private pleasure of hers, much as she could spend hours looking at how she could do this and that up on the machine and save all kinds of money, and wasn't that a great idea for a stall at the school bazaar?... Oooppps - danger. Wasn't that Edna pouring through the pattern books? I don't particularly want to get involved with Edna this morning. She's alright most days, but not this particular morning, not with the much needed item still unobtained, out there somewhere, elusive, a shadow in a corner of my mind - I'll just nip into leather goods here and she'll never see me. Aren't these purses nice? Real leather. Twenty-four pounds. You can always tell when its real leather, instant you touch it. Has a certain warmth about it. A bit steep though. Still, she could afford it. There was enough in her own simulated leather purse just now to afford it. She kept rolling it round in her hands, round and round, and felt the warmth of it, smelt its newness, its pure-leather-ness. Her eyes absentmindedly took in the arrangement of the aisle she was in, noting there was no one even remotely near. Her hand quickly and silently moved towards her coat pocket - yes, it was big enough. Just big enough. The leather purse fit snugly in. It felt good in there. She took a few stops forward. There, it's alright, the act of placing it in her well worn coat pocket seemed to change its character from *a* purse on the counter to *her* purse. It was satisfying... a little. And yet, it still wasn't what she sought. She had never done this sort of thing before, it had given her a type of thrill completely new, but it was short lived and by the time she left that department and got over into cosmetics, she felt nothing more than anxiety over not having obtained what she had come to town for, and had completely forgotten the leather purse. She looked worryingly at her watch. Just twenty minutes left! Panic swept over her body. Would she be able to find it in just twenty minutes? But she *had* to, she just *must*. Her hand flitted over the items in array - lipsticks, eye-shadows, hideous colours of nail varnish, compacts, very cheap and almost vulgar, then better ones, ones she had always fancied but never bought. The type you were proud to buy refills for. She picked one up. Tan, with mother-of-pearl, an unusual shape. Quicker than she realised, she had it in her pocket - the other one. That too seemed to be instantly hers. And it was so easy to do. But don't get distracted, she told herself. Keep on target. You might just miss what you came for. She must now be extremely efficient. There wasn't much time left. Her breathing became tense. She was like an overwound spring. Her movements were clumsy. The corner of her shopping bag caught the end of a display of eye-shadow pencils and sent them crashing to the ground. She bent, as if to pick them all up, then absently put just one into her pocket and carried on. It, whatever it was she had to have, was definitely here somewhere, she could sense it.

She felt a hand on her shoulder. It was strong, and firm, and cool, too. The voice was in character with the hand, calm and clear, not too loud but perfectly audible.

'We have reason to believe you may have been shop-lifting. Please would you accompany me to the manager's office - this way, madam,' the voice said.

She didn't even look at the face of the voice. She didn't feel the need to. Relief spread instantly all over her body, her muscles relaxed, the spring unwound. Like a robot she followed the store detective into an anonymous office. Drab tan walls with a drab tan carpet, and a very ordinary desk and two chairs.

Anonymous. Common. Entirely forgettable. But *she* wasn't anonymous anymore. Someone had noticed her, had picked her out. She was entirely uncommon and altogether important just now, and she felt a rush of blood through her veins. Margaret emptied the contents of her pockets on the desk, and allowed herself just a glimmer of a smile. It had taken some time, but at last - *this was it!* She had found what she came to town for!

Neither Power Nor Glory

by

Reginald Hunter

Damn it, I'm nearly asleep. I hate this rhythm when I'm tired... bompety-bomp... bompety-bomp... swing and sway... over the points... rock and roll... rock and roll... twist and shout... round the floor... hold her close... in my arms...

Hey! Wake up! Shake yourself! Lights coming up... keep her steady... slow down - now... passing the lights... into the station... and a nice... gentle... stop.

Usual faces, usual places. Always the same spot on the platform. Always the same bowler hats and striped trousers. Folded papers and rolled umbrellas. Never speaking, never smiling. All half asleep and not liking it one little bit. What a life! And they'll all be there again tonight in Town, waiting for me. Just as silent; just as tired; just as spruce; all keeping the stiff upper lip; all going home to the little woman and the tidy kids.

Sometimes I envy them. At least they get every evening off. Not like me. Odd hours off here and there, working when everyone else has finished. Still it's a good job and I like it, so be thankful. Nine till five like them would drive me potty.

Don't like these early turns though, especially after a bad night. Kid crying, wife moaning because I haven't mended that fence yet. Been edgy for some time now, she has. Complains she never sees me now-a-days. But if she wants all these modern gadgets like washing machines and coloured television, someone's got to earn the money. And to be fair, I want a video. She'd work if she could, I know, but she can't, not with the boy to look after.

Off again... speed up gently... musn't wake 'em up too soon! They might complain!... On time so far... watch for the crossing... sound the siren... bompety-bomp... bompety-bomp... Be passing the house soon. Wonder if she'll wave this morning? If she does I'll know everything's all right again. But I doubt it. Take her a couple of days to get over last night.

There was no need for it, either. I was just too tired. She expects me to do all these extra shifts to get the money, then grumbles if I'm too tired to do anything. I'll mend the damn fence. I shall have to 'cos it backs on to the line. But I'll do it in my own time when I feel like it - not when I'm told to. I won't be dictated to by anybody - and certainly not by a woman - not even the wife. She's the salt of the earth, but I wear the trousers in my house and that's how it's going to stay. Her job's to look after the boy - and at four he's handful enough, I should think. Takes after his Dad, he does. What he wants he gets...

It started when I got in last night. The boy had been tiresome all day she said. Got under her feet because she dare not put him out in the garden, she said, because of that damned hole. But he couldn't get through that. He's too big now. Besides he never plays at that end of the garden. All my vegetables are up that end, so there's nothing to attract him. I told her this, but she went on about it and I was tired.

Then he kept us awake most of the night crying. Some sort of colicky pain I think, that small kids sometimes get. We took turns walking up and down with him - for hours it seemed, before he cried himself to sleep. Then I slept so heavily I had to rush off this morning without any breakfast. Nobody's fault, I know - just one of those things that parents have to put up with now and then. He'll probably be as right as rain tonight. But it's spoilt both our tempers today.

No, she didn't wave when I passed. She wasn't there. Perhaps walked down to the station with some sandwiches for me. She's done that before. I'll keep an eye out when I stop.

Now shut up and concentrate. Missed my check point then. Should have started slowing down there. Must keep my mind on the job. Just have to brake a bit harder, that's all. Watch the lights now... now... slow... slow... bit more... bit more... Ah! Bet that jolted them out of their morning snoozes! Now... nice and smooth... nice and smooth... that's it... Practice and experience, that's what it is to keep a train under control... practice and experience.

Into the platform... gliding nicely... up to the board... slow right down... and a gentle... easy... stop.

There. Perfect.

No, she's not here. P'raps she's busy or gone out shopping or something - but why am I making excuses? She's obviously still ratty. Trying to hurt me. Well, she's not going to. Two can play at that game. I'll just ignore her.

Back again. Had a snack and a cup of tea in the canteen in Town. Feeling a bit better now. Three more runs. Three more times past my house, then I can put my feet up for a bit. Better do that fence first, though, I suppose. Put her mind at rest.

Here we go... bompety-bomp... bompety-bomp... wish I could wake up properly... sit up straight... it's the rhythm... the rhythm... the rhythm. Always the same... bompety-bomp... bompety-bomp... up line and down... down line and up... through the crossings... rounding the curves... watching the lights... bompety-bomp.

Under the bridge... kids on the top... dropping a stone... dangerous trick... I used to do - just the same... but steam engines then... puff-puff, puff-puff... lean over well... aim for the stack... great belch of smoke... covered in soot... marvellous fun... but dangerous now - with driver in front... bompety-bomp... bompety-bomp...

Station again... slowing down... shoppers this time... shoppers, school-kids and tourists... gentle approach... easy does it... and... stop.

I measure my day by the type of passengers that wait at the stations for me. The silent saturnine pin-striper first; then the housewives and school-kids; then the shoppers and day-trippers; then the same in reverse, going back home. Late shifts it's evening dresses and lounge suits, noisy parties and roisterous revellers.

Then the silence of the walk home. Supper and bed. Often don't see the boy at all. But she's always there, waiting for me. I shouldn't be so snappy with her, but I'm so damned tired these days.

The Romance of the Railways! Not from my angle. Just a tiring responsible job which has lost its glamour and excitement now. Just monotonous to-ing and fro-ing.

Be glad when my holiday comes round again. Twenty years of driving, both in steam and electric. Not bad. Plenty of people without jobs these days, so I should be thankful. Won't be long before I reach retirement. Be able to get down to some solid gardening then. Think I'll take an allotment. Then the wife can have all the garden for flowers and I can grow everything else we need. Shouldn't be difficult. Plenty of the old stagers from steam days have retired to allotments. I could join the Society. Keep me busy enough. Go in for competitions, too. See who can grow the biggest marrow and that sort of thing.

But that's five years away yet, all the time I can pass my medicals. Should do. I'm still pretty fit.

Hallo - there's my signal. Off again... mind on the job now... easy does it... bompety-bomp... passing the house again soon... will she be there this time? Think I've got some wood in the shed that'll do for the fence... bompety-bomp...

Sheet of paper on the line ahead. Somebody's lost his newspaper... no, it's a bundle of rag... No, can't be... What then?

My God! It's moving! It's alive! Crawling on the line! Opposite my house!... Opposite that fence!... God in Heaven - it's the boy! The boy!... and I can't stop!... God, I can't stop! Going too fast... God Almighty... Move, damn you, - move! Brakes... Power... Everything...!

Stop, you great bastard... stop!

Oh, my God, I can't. Coaches pushing... can't do a thing.

Twenty yards!

Crawl, you poor little sod... crawl! Crawl! Get off!... Get off!... Oh, dear God, have mercy!... Have pity!... Have pity!

Fifteen yards!

Helpless! Nothing I can do... poor little devil... For God's Sake... crawl!... Can't you hear me?... I can't do any more - I can't do any more...

Ten yards!

Forgive me - oh, forgive me! Dear God, forgive me!

What... ?

The wife... running... what's she doing?... Get back you fool - get back... you'll never do it! You fool - you brave, lovable fool!... I'll kill both of you... I can't stop... don't you understand? - I can't stop... oh... why don't you hear?...

Five yards!

She's gone! Oh, my God - she's gone... and the boy... I can't see her... I can't see anything... where is she... where is she?

Stopped. Stopped at last. But too bloody late... I can't move... don't ask me to look, please... I've killed her. I know I have... I've killed both of them... Oh, God... I can't move... please forgive... forgive...

Someone calling?

Not shouting or screaming?... Just calling... calling my name... can't be... can't be... too late... too late...

Oh, Thank God, Thank God...

She's safe... she's safe... and she's got the boy in her arms...

High Price for a High Rise

by

Gaye Giuntini

The child gazed from the grimy window of the flat in the high rise block where she had lived for most of her eight bleak years. The scream of London traffic joined with the city heat and rose to form a cobweb of dusty noise.

Cassie had been to the market that morning with her Mother to search for the cheapest cuts of meat from the flat-capped, fag-smoking fellow who was always shouting from his place between the fresh fish stall and the Indian selling jeans.

Chicken George, as Cassie had secretly named him after hearing something on the telly to do with roots and chickens, was a likeable bloke and always made time to have a chat with Cass and her Mum.

Cass couldn't remember the time when she had had a Dad to complete her family - Mum said that the bugger had scarpered soon after she was born, and they were better off without him anyway! Cassie wasn't too sure about this, although if some of her friends Dads were anything to go by, this may have been true!

Her very best friend, a pimply child named Jane, had awful stories to share, and most weeks would have a grim tale to tell Cass as they squatted amongst the litter which scarred the grass outside their estate.

'Me Dad got drunk again last night,' Jane said for the umpteenth time that month, 'he didn't 'arf wallop me Mum - she's all puffy and won't go outside!' Although Cassie was familiar with seeing bruises and bumps on many of the women in her neighbourhood, she had never seen any on her Mum - only eyes puffy and swollen from crying.

Everything was such a struggle - never enough money to buy clothes, except from that smelly jumble sale held every week in the Sally Army hall; never enough money to fill your stomach, except with chips; and *never* enough money to go to the countryside or the sea... except once.

Cass sat by the cracked window and remembered that day as clearly as the morning visit to the market. She was six and excited and couldn't wait to get on the huge green bus.

An outing to Margate had been organised by a local charity and the tickets included a picnic lunch and a stop for tea - the most exciting thing in the whole world! Her friend Jane was to be there with her Mother, and the two had planned loads of things to do on the beach... collect shells, dig through to Australia, (they hoped that a day would be long enough), swim if there weren't too many sharks about, and have a whole day away from the grimness of London life!

It began badly with the absence of Jane and her Mum due to the previous evening's booze-up and bashing! Cassie also wondered whether Jane had had another creepy visit from her Dad during the night - neither of them really understood why he kept doing it, but Jane was too frightened to push him away, or to tell her Mum. The girls often discussed this strange habit, but as Cassie had no Father of her own, they supposed that all grown-up men were allowed to do 'things'.

'I 'ate it when me Dad's been drinking,' Jane would say to Cassie 'e comes into my room and smells really awful - I get so scared but I daresn't call me Mum in case he 'its 'er again. I've only ever told you and it's a secret!'

Cassie had always kept the secret, but worried about her friend's tears.

She also worried a lot about her Mother's tears - there was a bleak desperation in every sob which came more and more frequently... a loneliness that Cass couldn't cure, not even when she cuddled next to her Mum in bed at night. Life seemed full of disappointment to the child, happiness came only in odd moments and dreams.

The memories faded a little now as Cassie wondered where her Mother was - she hadn't seen her since their return from the market when she had put their meagre meal on to simmer.

Strange, she thought, everything seems to be fading, the light from the street below, the light from the television flickering in the corner, the light from the dangling bulb above - even the colours in her jumble sale dress looked pale.

As she stared through the gloom she felt her Mother's cool touch on her hair, and heard the soft, sad voice saying, 'it's alright now, my darling... forgive me... I just couldn't go on. You'll be safe - you'll be happy.'

As they sat together, Cassie saw two figures lying on the street far below - familiar figures - one in a jumble sale dress...

The Brandenburger's Bones

by

Andrew Bowers

John Draco turned and walked away from the knot of people standing silently among the grass covered dunes. The sea hissed gently against the sandy beach and a lark rose singing into the sky. John was glad to have witnessed the unearthing of the skeleton, not for any ghoulish reason but for the uproar its discovery was going to bring about. Of those present, John alone knew that these bones should never have been found here at all.

John happened to be on the beach when he spotted police cordoning off a small area in the dunes and edging back a group of bystanders. He had rushed to join them and saw the bones as they were dug out of the sand and taken away. The skull was shattered at the front as if struck by a bullet and someone thought that the remains were those of a murder victim.

John saw the tattered field grey uniform clinging to the mouldy bones and knew that this person had not been unlawfully killed. These were the remains of a German soldier killed in 1940 during an attack on the Kent coast.

For twenty five years now, John had been collecting evidence to show that on or about 7th September 1940, Germany had carried out a commando-style raid on the south coast of England. All the 'experts' had scornfully dismissed this evidence and denounced John in no uncertain terms. Today all that would change, for here was proof that could not be explained away.

On the television news that evening the man who made the discovery described how a buckle on the uniform had activated his metal detector. He said he'd scoured that particular area many times before without finding anything important.

'It's weird,' the man said, speaking in the self-conscious tone the ordinary adopt when unwanted fame is thrust upon them. 'All the time I've wandered that beach and found nothing and now this. It's incredible.'

'It's a very interesting discovery,' Arthur Zollern, an historian told his interviewer. 'But it's too early to say for sure if it is a genuine German soldier.'

'What do you mean, 'genuine'?' the interviewer asked.

'Well,' Zollern replied, 'it might be someone murdered while dressed as a German soldier. A member of a World War Two re-enactment society, for example.'

John grinned at this. The pictures these 'experts' paint to avoid rewriting the history books!

Naturally the event was first item on the local news programme as well. The Sevenoaks grave robbery, which had dominated these past few days, was pushed into a poor second place.

The newspapers next day were full of the story and pressure was growing on the government to release all the official records from 1940. Some of these were still classified after fifty years and set to remain so for many years yet.

The media arrived to ask John for his opinion of the affair. He told them he was glad that from now on he would no longer be denounced as a crackpot and pseudo-historian.

John watched himself on the news that night which also carried interviews with several other people who were connected with the skeleton. It was revealed that the dead man was from an elite unit, the Brandenburgers, trained to operate behind enemy lines, to capture or demolish bridges and fortifications. This training was carried out on an estate near Brandenburg, hence the name.

This was a mystery to everyone who claimed to be an expert on the Second World War. Why would Brandenburgers have been sent to this part of the coast, which was devoid of any strategic buildings or bridges? Wherever the Brandenburgers went the main German army followed shortly afterwards, so why had no other skeletons been discovered?

John was puzzled as well for he thought Brandenburgers had also carried out hit and run raids like commandos. The first tiny inkling that something had gone terribly wrong stirred within him.

People came forward claiming to have been in Kent at the time and an old soldier told of a brief gun battle with about twenty Germans. Apparently the main invasion never made it to England but small groups of Germans had attacked the Kent coast that night. The soldier told how his unit killed a German and buried him in secret after a brief religious ceremony. The men were ordered never to tell of the incident for fear of the news creating panic amongst the population. According to the soldier this occurred in the first week of September 1940, exactly as John had claimed.

Several experts announced that the skeleton was genuine, an invasion had been attempted and the history books would have to be rewritten. At last, John was winning his long battle although the government maintained a stern silence which worried him. If only the secret files were made public then everything will have been worth it.

Within a week of the find doubts were cast upon the skeleton's authenticity. The skull had been smashed, not by a bullet but by a projectile fired from close range from an unknown weapon. What was most puzzling was the fact that the skull had been shattered many years after the man's death. Why would anyone break a dead man's skull?

John was arrested a week later when the hoax had been fully exposed. He confessed immediately telling the police that the skeleton was the one taken from the tomb in Sevenoaks. He had fired a ball-bearing from a catapult into the skull at point-blank range in order to shatter it in the way a bullet would.

John's motive had been to force the government to release the sealed files concerning the attempted invasion. Following this, he would have confessed to the skeleton hoax and calmly accepted the consequences, happy with the knowledge that he was right and everybody else wrong.

His secondary objective, which he had largely achieved, was to ruin the reputation of the experts who had for so long derided his invasion theory.

'What about the other skeleton?' one of the grim-faced policemen asked.

'What other skeleton?' John asked. 'I only did the one.'

'Well,' the policeman replied, 'our colleagues in Dover found another set of bones yesterday, a paratrooper this time. Tell us what you know about this one.'

'I know nothing,' John said. 'Nothing whatsoever, I assure you.'

The Dark Red Rose

by

Yoni

Ernst suddenly found himself in the German army, it all seemed to have happened overnight somehow. A few days ago he'd been busy on his father's farm and now he had a rifle instead of a pitchfork. He looked at himself in the mirror, yes the uniform was smart, no doubt about that but the very sight of it brought fear into his heart, fear for Sarah. He'd known Sarah for some while. When his father bought the farm, Sarah's family owned the adjacent farm but the big problem was they were Jewish. Things had been getting progressively hot for Jews and just lately the all-out hunt for them was in force. They'd already just lost their shops, business, farms, homes and only the other week a family had disappeared not so far away.

Sarah's heart nearly stopped when she met Ernst for the first time in his uniform for that uniform roused panic in all Jewish hearts.

'You must not see me any more Ernst,' she told him falteringly with tears in her eyes. 'It will only get you into trouble. Anyway I expect we'll be taken away next.'

'I will hide you in the attic...'

'No no I will not let you and your family be in such danger. Don't worry about us, if we must suffer with our people then so be it.'

'You are very brave Sarah. I've seen Jews terrified when about to be rounded up, searching desperately for a refuge and I've hated having to be amongst those doing these things but I will not just leave you open to this danger. Do you realise what they'll do with you? There's no mercy in those satanists and if I can help it they'll not have you.'

After that meeting Ernst returned from his leave of duty. His melancholy caused his mates to chide him saying he must be in love but what, he wondered, would they say if they knew what she was? It didn't bear thinking about so he told them nothing. Let them think what they liked.

A few weeks later Sarah had gone into the woods around the farm, having finished the work for that morning. She often went there, not only because she loved the woods but it was a good source of firewood as well. She was thankful that they were isolated like this as they'd been left alone, so far anyway. However her thankfulness was short lived when she heard the lorry coming, then raucous voices as guards jumped from the vehicle bawling to the inmates to come out. They crashed into the house and returned dragging her parents.

'Where's the girl?' demanded one. 'You have a daughter, where is she?'

Sarah couldn't hear the words but she got the gist of it. When her parents were in the lorry, the soldiers began hunting for her around the outhouses and barns. Sarah stood frozen to the spot as she peered through the trees. After a while they gave up and went off storming about... 'getting her next time...'

She felt too numb to cry, only angry guilt with herself, she should have gone with them, now she'd never see Mother and Father again. With trepidation she returned to the house and when she saw the things scattered and broken all over the place she then burst into tears. She went out to the byre and shed more tears on Gretchen's soft hide. The big cow turned and looked at her with dark soulful eyes.

'Oh what will happen to you all when they come for me?' she said between sobs. Gretchen gave a deep moo and went on chewing.

Ernst's base was not far away and he'd been put to guard the railway junction. So it wasn't long before he heard what had happened at the farm.

'That place is next to your place isn't it?' enquired one of his mates. When he nodded the speaker went on: 'How can you bear to live near a bunch of Jews?'

'We didn't know who they were, they've never bothered us,' answered Ernst trying desperately hard to keep his temper.

He must somehow get up there and find out what had become of Sarah. When he was due for a few hours off he made a bee-line for the farm but couldn't find Sarah anywhere. On his way to his own farm he heard his name being called and Sarah came running out from the trees. She flung her arms round his neck and smothered him with tearful kisses.

'Oh Ernst, they've taken Mum and Dad.'

'I know I know. That's why I've come as soon as I could to find out what was happening to you.'

'Your father has been good to me, he comes every day to help with the animals but I'm frightened for him. Oh what shall I do? Maybe I should give myself up.'

'Never never. Don't say such things.' He calmed her down. 'Dad will take the animals to his farm then you needn't worry for him. I'll sort it out.'

They walked back to his farm keeping well into the trees then skirted round by the hedge.

'There's an old loft over the cowshed that's never been used,' he told her. 'You may stay up there and if they come round asking about you there's a door at the back with some steps leading down. Come I'll show you.'

'I'll not go far though, their dogs will soon finish me. Then they'll punish your father...'

'We'll think of something anyway.'

After he'd made her comfortable in the loft he went down to the village. When he returned he presented her with a bunch of luscious red roses.

'I'll have to go back now, I only have a few hours off. What ever you do, *keep out of sight.*'

When he'd gone Sarah put the roses in a bowl and thought how wonderful it would be if there were no war and no maniacs like Hitler in the world. She cared for those roses tenderly for to her they were Ernst. She changed their water frequently and often caressed their soft velvet petals. Now that her animals were all with Ernst's father she didn't have to worry about going to her farm so much.

As the days went by the roses gradually faded and one by one they were discarded which was a pity for it was like discarding Ernst. Also there'd been peace around, no more raiding and it began to look as though they'd be left alone.

One morning was a beautiful sunny one and as usual all appeared peaceful. Surely there was no need now to keep up such vigilance she hadn't been to her farm since Ernst had visited. She'd like to see the old farmhouse again and maybe spend a little time there although it would be sad. The roses were now down to the last one and this particular one was the deepest red and it seemed as though it refused to die. This one was the last of Ernst and she carefully lifted it out of the pot.

'I'll take it to the farm with me,' she said to herself. 'It'll be like going back with Ernst.'

The day was so lovely she forgot about all the evils around, she wished this day would last forever. On approaching the empty byre and house she felt a pang of sadness for her parents but who knew, maybe they'd all meet again some day. She opened the door and went into the silent kitchen. For some while she sat by the window watching the fields. Suddenly she was awakened from her reverie by the noise of an engine. In panic she made for the cellar, still clutching her rose and dropped the trapdoor behind her. She crouched behind the barrels as she heard heavy boots crash through the door above and clomp into the kitchen. Her heart sank when she heard the dogs. She had been right for the dogs soon made short work of her. Still clutching the rose she was pulled and kicked into the lorry.

Ernst was on guard duty at the junction when he heard a commotion back at the station. He saw prisoners being herded into wagons, with shouting and bawling they were crammed in and the doors shut. The train started off. As it approached he noticed a face at the barred window.

'Ernst!' shouted a voice.

His blood froze when he heard his name. As the train passed on a hand came through the bars and threw something. When the train had gone he marched slowly up to the spot where whatever it was had fallen. He wept when he saw the single dark red rose.

A Talent for Deception

by

Robert Fish

Malcolm Grislin had not been particularly successful. His short and rather undistinguished career ended the night an unconvinced audience chanted for their money back in the company of a small but influential group of record producers. Malcolm was not of star quality but he felt he had good reason to be bitter. Not only did he feel subject to the mismanagement of agent Sam Mason but also mislead by his hypnotic voice which seemed to constantly echo the words 'You're goiner be a hit my friend, just stay with me'. The mere thought that stardom was about to be realised made Malcolms mouth water in belief of this comical entertainment cliché.

Of course, stardom was not about to be realised for poor old Malcolm Grislin. By the time that fateful evening at the 'Cabaret à Paris' had ended and the candles blown out, he was driving home, drowning in his own self pity and reflecting on a closed contract with those elusive words still ringing in his ears 'You're goiner be a hit my friend just stay with me'. It was of no surprise that Malcolm was not in the best of moods. A mood which wasn't helped by the thought that those hazy images of stardom had represented an escape route from Malcolms already fragile marriage. There were to be no high society women flocking at his feet, not tonight. All there seemed to exist was the long dark road taking him home into a life of certain obscurity.

Unawares to Malcolm, the most significant part of his disappointment was linked to the striking resemblance that he had with his agent. A likeness so close to his that on numerous occasions during their brief working relationship they had been mistaken. However, Sam Mason was successful, Malcolm was not. This was essentially the route to Malcolms bitterness, someone so similar in features exuded power and influence where Malcolm was simply a failure.

It was at this point, when all these emotions were turning themselves over in his head that the dashboard on his car went dim, the engine seemed to die on him instantly and the modest car which he had visions of replacing ground to a halt.

After attempting to start the car in vain two of three times he opened the door, stepped out into the mild winter night and lifted up the bonnet. After looking randomly at the mass of components and wires he quickly admitted defeat and retreated back to the car to contemplate his next move. His train of thought didn't last long before he found himself reflecting again. It wasn't long after five minutes that Malcolm was disturbed by a startling light of a car driving around the slight bend in the road. The car drove past and made that distinctive noise of a vehicle passing you at a high speed on a quiet stretch. There was nothing quite like the feeling of complete inertia which such a noise instils. Malcolm drifted back into despair.

And then, the noise of that car which had disappeared into the distance could be heard again. It was reversing back to where Malcolm was situated, but it didn't seem to interfere with his trance. The driver stepped out of the car, walked over to Malcolms window and knocked with the vigour of an impatient man. Malcolm looked up and to his complete surprise and horror it was him, Sam Mason, with that look on his face which seemed to pierce through the darkness. Malcolm wound down the window.

'That you Grislin?' Malcolm didn't answer. 'What you doing here pulled up?' Mason persisted and then stopped silent for a moment, drew back a sigh then added... 'You don't wanner give up hope just yet Mal, there's plenty of people I can still talk to about giving you some time in the studio, Rome wasn't built in a day, you just stay with me...' Malcolm intercepted at this point to prevent Mason saying those infamous last words...

'It's the car, I'm fine really.' This was not true. Malcolm was not fine. In fact, at this point all he felt was anger, particularly at this untimely meeting with the man who had just ended his dream with false promises and silky smiles.

That was the turning point for Malcolm. Mason was just starting towards his bonnet when Malcolm s emotions accumulated into a vision more cunning and terrible than he had ever considered. Could it be possible to kill Mason here and now, in the darkness of this road and take on his life? It would only take one possibly two blows to the head and Sam Mason would be dead. Surely it would only be a case of replacing his body with Masons in the driving seat and pushing the car down the embankment at the side of the road. It was the complete scenario; Malcolm Grislin, failure in life and marriage would be dead, a freak accident, possibly suicide. He would live as Sam Mason, devastated at the tragic death of his friend and colleague.

That was all it took for Malcolm to justify his actions. His was obviously out of control of his emotions. There was nothing to lose and at that point Malcolm actually felt he had the ability to take someone's life. He grabbed the bar like lock which protected the car from theft and glanced up to Mason. Mason was shouting something from the bonnet but Malcolm didn't pay any attention as he opened the door and moved towards Mason. Just at the time Mason was about to shout again some instructions, Malcolm Grislin had done it. It had only taken thirty seconds at the most between the decision to murder and the actual crime. A second blow was needed and Malcolm in an almost maniac spell carried out his work.

For such a spontaneous idea the following weeks passed with considerable ease for Malcolm Grislin, now Sam Mason. The procedure of adopting Masons disposition was not a difficult job to undertake. He had always been predictable in speech as well as actions. It was not long before he was mastering those great lines and echoing them to any fresh faced talent that may walk through his door.

The greatest success for Malcolm was the ability to deal with his own conscience. Not only did he feel little remorse for his actions and the effect that it would have on his heart broken wife, but also the nerve to help organise his own funeral with her. Moreover, he confidently dealt with police enquiries into the mental state of the late Mr Grislin before his death. The verdict: accident, case closed.

Malcolm Grislin was now convinced his crime would never be revealed. His was adapting to his new way of life, Mrs Grislin was coming to terms with her loss, life was tasting sweeter than it ever had done. However, what Malcolm didn't account for was the wallet belonging to Sam Mason had been accidentally dropped as he changed into the clothes of Masons at the scene of the murder. This incriminating evidence would imply that Sam Mason had been there at the incident, suggesting that this was a murder enquiry rather than an accident. Unfortunately for Malcolm this vital piece of evidence was discovered by a curious young detective desperate to impress his seniors. The detective had returned to the site since he was convinced that the minimal damage incurred on the car implied that it had been pushed rather than driven down the embankment at high speed.

The discovery of the wallet had changed everything within days. The case was reopened with Sam Mason the prime suspect in the murder of Malcolm Grislin. Malcolm still play acting in Sam Masons office was completely unaware of the latest development and continued to sit proudly in his new office. Unfortunately he was playing the acting part too well. Everyone believed he was Sam Mason, agent to the stars, but soon everyone was to believe he was Sam Mason, murderer of Malcolm Grislin.

The twist of fate was only going to be briefly realised for Malcolm. Before long poor Mrs Grislin had been informed of the arrest being made, and without hesitation took one of three ornamental rifles attached to the fireplace. She would make the man who had killed her husband feel the pain that he had felt.

Malcolm Grislin didn't even enter custody before he came face to face with his wife. Time had no true quantity now. He had enough moments to grasp the images of the last few weeks but not the time to make some weak cry of innocence. Before the officers could stop Mrs Grislin a bullet had made contact with Malcolms chest. Malcolm Grislin was dead, the architect of his own murder.

A Time Share Break

by

C D Doran

Andrew and Joan Littlewood, scarcely commented on the name of the cafe before going in. To call an honest to goodness, quayside, transport type of cafe the 'Bistro', was perhaps not extravagantly incongruous, but this was Campbeltown, a quiet, almost redundant Scottish fishing port not Marseilles waterfront. As it turned out, the 'Bistro' was to provide one of two more surprises before the Littlewoods were even properly inside.

Firstly, although the premises were clearly open for business, and there were already customers inside, the door presented unexpected resistance. Andrew had to push hard to open it, and no sooner were he and his wife inside, than the door sprang from his grasp and crashed to with a force that made all the windows rattle, and an item of cutlery on a nearby table fall to the floor. Andrew received the expected stony look from Joan and then looked about guiltily, ready with his apologies. They did not seem necessary, however, as nobody appeared to have noticed, not even the young woman who was busy wiping the tables.

With a solid breakfast of eggs, bacon and a mug of stewed tea before them, Andrew and Joan settled to planning their day. The Littlewoods were an unremarkable couple in their forties, who ran a news agents in South London. They had arrived at Campbeltown in the early morning as the first part of a tour of Scotland in their motor caravan. It was their first ever visit to Scotland, and though an ordinary down to earth couple, it was a certain romance in their souls which had brought them to the Kintyre peninsula in the first place.

Andrew as a long time Paul McCartney fan wanted to visit the Mull of Kintyre, whereas Joan said, 'I want to see the cave painting of the Crucifixion on the island.'

What? I thought cave paintings were supposed of pre-historic, in which case the crucifixion would not be a subject.

'This was painted by a Scottish artist called ...' She referred to a guide book 'Archibold Mackinnon in eighteen eighty seven, then he returned some years later to retouch it. It's in a cave on the South shore of Davaar Island in Campbeltown Loch.'

Andrew did not really share Joan's fascination for the distant past, but was, however, looking forward to his moment, when he could stand in the footsteps of the great Paul McCartney.

Referring to her guide book again, Joan said 'You can only cross to the island at low tide when the cause way is passable. Are you coming with me?' Joan knew he would decline but did not really mind. This was a private quest, best enjoyed in the company of no one.

'No I don't think so. I'll take you along to the causeway, drop you off and then come back into town for a while and pick up a few things. How long do you think you'll be?'

'Come and pick me up in about two hours. If we miss each other, I'll make for this cafe and I expect we'll meet up eventually.'

And so it was agreed, and they left the cafe. Andrew drove his wife to the causeway, which was almost a mile along the straight road.

'See you back here in two hours,' called Andrew as he drove off.

As Joan made her way towards the island, the sea was still only just relinquishing the causeway, and here and there, she found herself actually wading and getting her feet very wet in the process. She did not want to wait any longer for the tide, as that would cut into her precious two hours. She did not know how long it would take to get to the island, or if when she did, she could even find the cave. When she eventually arrived, she realised she did not know which way to turn, left or right. On the south shore the guide book said, but which way was south. Her appalling ignorance of the most elementary principle of navigation, meant that she had to rely on intuition or just trust to luck. She turned right.

The shore line was very rocky, and there seemed to be no reasonable stretch where she could walk normally, but instead stumbled, leapt and even at times crawled over the rocks. Periodically, she came on a cave, which she searched thoroughly. When she had drawn a blank for the third time, Joan was beginning to wonder, had her instinct let her down, and she should have gone the other way round.

She calculated, that it might just be possible to circumnavigate the island in the time, and so more in hope than confidence, she continued on her way.

The very next cave she came to, looked no more likely to be the one than any of the others, less so in fact, but she discovered that it was two caves with a narrow opening joining the two. When the first cave yielding nothing, she scrambled through the opening, banging her head as she passed. She thought she was out of luck again, and was about to leave through the second cave entrance, when she saw it above the gap she had just come through.

Joan was not at all sure what her reaction should have been at the sudden revelation. There was no burst of the Hallelujah Chorus, the light was not good, so no miraculous beam of sunlight to illuminate the painting, and she was not sure the painting was even very good. Nevertheless, Joan was entranced.

She stood motionless, letting her thoughts flow freely into the past, looking over the shoulder fo the aged artist, as he restored the work of his youth. The spell was gradually unravelled, as she went on to consider the more mundane problem of how the work had been preserved for so long in this damp environment. After a time she looked at her watch and decided that the fifteen minutes she had spent in the cave was enough, and set off back the way she had come.

When Joan reached the causeway, she looked towards the mainland, and breathed a sigh of relief when she saw the camper was not at the agreed meeting place. She could walk, without hurry and without any feeling of guilt at keeping Andrew waiting. When she reached the mainland, and there was still no sign of her husband, the relief she felt earlier was replaced by a mild irritation, which grew steadily as the minutes ticked by with still no sign of him. Three quarters of an hour later Joan gave up and seething steadily, headed for the 'Bistro'.

With still no sign when she arrived, she went in, and her anger carried through the resistant door with ease. As with Andrew earlier, however, the door slipped from her grasp and crashed violently so that she thought it must break every window in the place, Once again, nobody so much as flinched. Joan settled at a table where she had a good view of the door. After ordering a meal she picked up a newspaper from the seat beside her, but she was unable to absorb anything she read, as her mind was constantly on her errant husband. Every so often the door would release itself from some unsuspecting grasp and she would look up expecting Andrew, only to see some sheepish stranger looking guiltily about them.

Her meal over, the coffee drunk and little excuse left to remain on the premises Joan prepared to leave. At that moment Andrew came through the door.

Andrew looked round the cafe and seemed about to leave when he caught sight of Joan. He released the door, which crashed shut with its accustomed vigour, that up ended a salt cellar on an adjacent table. He stood transfixed and Joan glared back. Joan noticed that he had changed his clothes which added suspicion to an already angry state. Andrew approached the table hesitantly without taking his eyes from her face, and sat opposite her.

'Where the hell have you been? You should have picked me up over two hours ago.'

'Joan.' He stopped unable to continue.

'Joan.' Again he stopped, while his wife continued to glower, determined not to give an inch as he tried to work out his excuses.

'Joan, I've been back on this day every year for the past three years, since you disappeared.'

Forced to Run

by

Richard Nairn

He pushed his way through the last of the trees and bushes, to see the murky waters of the river, lying still in the cold air.

To his right he saw the bridge towering high, or so it seemed, and he could hear the cars speeding over it.

As he staggered along the dry mud bank towards the end of the bridge, he realised he would have to cross it as quickly as possible, in case anyone he knew recognised him in such a public place.

Mark was seventeen and wasn't completely sure what he was doing, although he was sure he didn't want to go back. Not back, not there, he couldn't bear to think of the trouble he would get in for what he had done.

It wasn't his fault. He hadn't meant to do it. It was just that, that boy had gone too far.

'You're the biggest bloody wimp I've ever met,' the boy had said.

Mark had been sitting on the sea wall at the time, staring up at the boy standing next to him. As the boy started kicking him in the ribs, Mark's eyes welled up with tears and he had felt the anger building up inside of him.

'Thud' the pain spread up Mark's side and he had automatically pushed at his offenders legs to make him retreat. The boys legs twisted around, and as Mark had stared in horror, he had disappeared over the edge of the wall, screaming.

He hadn't meant to do it, he had just been pushed too far, and now he had to leave. After seeing the body lying on the floor three metres below, blood upon his forehead, Mark had to run. Was he unconscious, or dead? Mark didn't know, maybe he didn't want to, but all he intended to do was get as far away as possible.

He arrived at the end of the bridge, his clothes clinging to his body and his heart beating rapidly.

He started to cross. The cars drove past him, people didn't seem to be paying him any attention. He walked on to the end of the bridge and looked back at where he had come from. He breathed a sigh of relief and walked off the edge of the road.

In the trees beside the motorway he found a clear patch on which he sat down. He took out a chocolate bar from his pocket and took a bite from it then put it back. Mark yawned, and lay back in the damp grass and closed his eyes, listening to the steady hum of the traffic speeding by behind him. The noise didn't bother him, he was too tired.

He awoke a while later as the horn of a car blared past. After getting up and rubbing his eyes, he walked back out to the side of the road, hoping he might be able to hitch a lift, provided he was careful no-one he knew drove past.

The cars just kept passing by one by one, until finally a little blue mini slowed down until it was nearby.

The driver was an old man with a thick white moustache wearing a cap.

He leaned out and said in friendly tones, 'A young man like you shouldn't be hitch hiking,' and then after a short pause 'Well come on, in yer get.'

They drove in silence for a while until finally,

'Got a name?' asked the old man.

No reply.

'Oh, you're a quiet one are you?' he exclaimed, 'I'll put the radio on for you.'

The old man turned on the radio, and the news came over rather crackly.

'A teenager was found today with head injuries and is...'

The radio was turned over by the man and some opera music filled the car. It was raining now, quite hard.

'Things are looking pretty dismal, aren't they?' said the old man, trying to start a conversation.

'They are for me,' said Mark as he stared out of the window at the gloominess, which reminded him of life.

Both Sides of the Coin

by

Edith Wynne-Williams

I looked up from the menu I was studying to find her standing in front of me. Immediately I was transported back more than a century, a period I had great empathy with. The girl before me was Jane Eyre, Shirley, Lucy Snowe. I blinked, thinking I was dreaming, but no, she stood looking at me her pad in one hand, pencil poised above it in the other. Demure, petite, in black skirt and plain white blouse. Her rounded features enhanced the deep set eyes. Her small rosebud mouth broke into a smile as she spoke, but it was her hair, soft mouse brown, drawn back, plaited and coiled at the nape of her neck - she had stepped straight out of a Bronte Novel.

Pulling myself together, I ordered steak pie, the 'veg of the day', jam roll and custard. My eyes followed her as she turned and walked up the dining room, between the round oak tables, towards the kitchen. I found them glued to the door for her re-entry. This was ridiculous I thought and unfolded my newspaper to read whilst waiting for my meal to arrive. Each time the kitchen door swung open my eyes darted over the top of my paper. The other waitresses came and went. I waited. I didn't want to miss a moment of her walk through the restaurant with my meal. At last she emerged, her longish skirt swirling round her legs as she stepped down from the upper dining area to the lower one where I was seated. My eyes followed her every movement. She placed the plate in front of me. I smiled and thanked her. She smiled back. I had noticed she had no ring on the third finger of her left hand. My mind was in a whirl. I scarcely tasted the meal as I devoured it. She collected my empty plate and returned to the kitchen to fetch the jam roll. Again I watched her progress to and from the kitchen, utterly fascinated. By the time I had finished my pudding I was in love with her. I wanted to hire a coach and horses, drive out into the night with her. Carry her into a hostelry, place her gently on the four-poster. My mind stopped there - I didn't know the girl, how could I let a hairstyle so affect me. My obsession with the Nineteenth century novel was getting out of hand - this was 1992. That evening I waited for her as she left the restaurant. She shut the door behind her and moved in my direction. She saw me. We moved towards each other - but she was a different girl. Her hair was loose and flowing, her outdoor skirt was above her knees, eye-shadow and lipstick coloured her face. As we passed I raised my hat. 'Good evening,' I said.

I knew he fancied me, I could always tell, felt their eyes upon me as I tripped back and forth to the kitchen. His were a penetrating blue. As I walked up the room I could feel him mentally undressing me. It had often occurred to me to do a strip-tease, discarding first the crockery, then my clothes, in an exotic dance, escaping through the kitchen door at the crucial moment. But this one was a little different and younger. Not like the usual old philanderer who came in for coffee and a gape. Men, I shall never understand them - think they're God's gift to women - if only they knew!

I'd marked him down as a solid steak and pie man, and that's exactly what he ordered. When I'm bored, I play this little guessing game. Sometimes even order the dish before they've decided - work a sort of telepathy on them. Well, it makes life more interesting.

He left me a generous tip - they usually did. Perhaps they felt a bit guilty of their naughty thoughts - a sort of mental infidelity to 'the little woman' at home. What a ghastly expression!

My feet ached and I was glad to see the last of the customers depart. Quickly, I changed, shook my hair free, brushed it vigourously. I don't think it liked being restrained but the management were a bit fussy of flowing locks. I suppose they were right, I wouldn't like to find a hair in my custard.

My freedom was the other side of the door. I wrenched it open, skipped outside and turned the key. Turning right I set off down the road. My God, 'steak pie' was waiting for me, starting to come towards me. What shall I do? I can't change direction.

Some paces from me he raised his hat and said 'Good evening'. I could see he wasn't going to stop. I grinned broadly and returned his greeting. Men!

Going for Gold

by

Michael Smith

The old man looked thoughtfully out at the open country before him as he considered the boy's question. His eyes squinted at the harsh glare of the Californian sunshine and a smile played on his lips as he removed his pipe.

'You want to know how an old fool like your grandpappy got to be so wealthy?' he said, giving his own rendition of the question and directing an affectionate glance at the freckle faced boy who sat beside him on the porch. He then returned his steadfast gaze to the fields as though they were holding a mirror to his past.

'I wasn't much older than nineteen when I got a keen itch to go in search for gold. I'd heard stories of that yellow ore that could fill a library. Stories of men who took to the hills and months later returned with mules packed down with gold. I saw it once myself - I'd swear those critters looked shorter in the legs for it.'

He paused in order to relight his pipe then, blowing out the flame, continued. 'There were others of course, who weren't so lucky. Bushwhackers, feuding between partners, snake bites, or just plum madness left them wasted as spent bullets. But if you made it back with your heart still a thumping and your mule bags fatter than a turkey on Christmas Eve, well you were home and free and there wasn't a man in town who wouldn't want to shake your hand or stand you a drink. Money might buy friendship - but gold, that could win over even your enemies! Well I'd heard enough to convince me I was a sap stopping where I was. My brother Jeff felt the same way as I did but my ma and pa weren't seeing us eye to eye and were agin' us going. 'Gold is for fools and kings', pa would say eyeing me up and down, 'And you don't look like any Prince I knowed'. Jeff and I weren't put off, we figured ma and pa would see our side once they saw the gold in our possession. We planned to creep away when they were asleep. We took the one mule and the supplies I'd prepared the night before and Jeff took pa's hunting rifle and some cartridges. I left a note on the table, it read 'we're coming back kings'.

for more weeks than I could count we dragged and pushed our mule under a blistering sun - that beast had four legs but she didn't seem to want to use any of them -'

'What about the gold Grandfather, when did you find the gold?' interrupted the boy his eyes set to pop in anticipation.

'It was after the night of the storm. I've never seen one like it before or since, it rained so hard I thought my hat was being nailed to my head. The thunder made our mule so fidgety we were afraid that she would bring the tree she was tied to down on us. Towards daybreak the storm had passed and the sun was smiling through.

I was squeezing the last vestige of rain from my hat and got to thinking that maybe pa was right and prospecting was for fools when suddenly Jeff let out an almighty yelp. I thought the rain had shrunk his breeches until I'd seen what he was hollering about. He was bent on his knees and scooping up mud in his hat, and as I drew closer to see what had stirred his excitement he gently parted the mud with his fingers and with my heart going like a pony express I saw the unmistakable twinkle of gold. Well you could have heard us whoop with joy if you'd been standing clear into Texas. We were high with fever dancing and laughing as we filled our hats with the treasure at our feet.

For days after that we lived with pans in our hands and a yellow gleam in our eyes. We didn't mind the hard work, two happier men I'm sure you couldn't have found. Even our mule was content because she didn't have to go no place.'

The story teller hesitated as if on a stumbling block but the silence urged him on.

'Then I got took with fever - not gold fever but fever fever. Jeff tried to nurse me as best he knew how but I became worse and Jeff told me he was going to fetch help.

He left me a canteen of water and the last I saw of my brother he was heading down the track with pa's rifle. I don't know how long I'd lain there but when you're sick time don't mean much. I'd barely enough strength to lift the canteen to my lips but thirst can pop a muscle when your desperate.

Well I thought I was done for and that's a fact, if those Quakers hadn't shown up when they did, well I wouldn't be sitting here now. All I can remember is waking up in a bed with sheets so clean I was afraid to touch them and I could see canvas in four corners and then I knowed I was in a wagon.

First thing that came into my head was that Jeff had brought help. I was set to call him when the canvas parted and a man in a black suit stepped inside. I must have shown my disappointment because he asked me if I was expecting my brother. Then I knew he's seen Jeff because we were twins.'

The old man brushed away a tear and his voice trembled with emotion.

'The Quakers found my brother with a bullet in his back, I guess it was scavengers who done it. Those people buried him and said prayers though they never knowed him. It was the buzzards who led those good folk to me.

I owed a heap to those Quakers and as soon as I was strong and on my feet I went to the mule to give them some of the gold Jeff and I had worked so hard for. My hands had hardly touched the animal when I saw the gold was gone. It didn't take long in figuring out where it had got to. Jeff knew I was poor protection for all that gold, being flat on my back with fever and all, so he'd buried it, like he were banking money. Truth was, the gold no longer mattered, I wasn't going to go turning over rock and soil to find it; when you've lost something as valuable as kinfolk everything else doesn't figure - the gold was 'buried' when Jeff died.

The Quakers left later that day and before heading home myself I went to Jeff's grave where I stood shaking as emotion poured down my cheeks. Then with my eyes still burning I walked on downhill with my mule in tow.

Seven weeks later I was back home putting up a fence on my pa's land. My folks showed no ill will towards me for running off like I did: ma embraced me so tight I'd thought my anatomy would fold in. Pa kept pumping my hand like he were drawing water from it.

I'd never felt so good as I did then catching sight of smoke curling up from the house as I swung down a mallet onto the fence post.

I brought that weight down so hard that when I first saw the dark liquid seeping to the surface I'd thought I'd done bled the ground -'

'What was it Grandpa?' the boys eyes looked like they were set to leave his face.

The storyteller put his pipe back into his mouth before speaking.

'Black gold.'

Death by Dust

by

Avril Barwick

'You passed your phobia onto the boys,' my husband said to me over breakfast recently.

And I couldn't argue with him because we both remember the day I screamed as I walked into the living room to see our twenty-one inch television screen bulging with spider legs.

The programme was 'Doctor Who', an episode involving friendly, intelligent, mild-mannered, English-speaking, giant spiders. The one that I glimpsed had a gentle female voice. I wasn't fooled for a minute of course. All we arachnophobics know spiders are mean and menacing.

I had been leading number one son by the hand into the room because he had wandered into the kitchen, which was very odd. This was his time with Daddy. Every Saturday evening both sons, then aged three and four, would settle in front of the television with their dad to watch 'Doctor Who', and I would escape to the kitchen.

'What's the matter?' I said as I took him by the hand. 'Come on darling, this is your time with daddy, isn't it?'

He just continued to suck his two middle fingers and allowed himself to be led back to the living room.

And then I screamed. God forgive me. I screamed, just the once, but loud and heartfelt, in front of our sons, at the sight of that silly, synthetic spider. I regretted it instantly, but the scream was out and couldn't be taken back. I tried to gloss over it:

'Silly Mummy. Is that a spider? ohhh... that's alright then. I thought it was a scorpion...'

Pathetic.

I really wanted sons who would grow up without my fear of spiders. Partly for their own sakes and partly because two extra rescuers in the house would be very handy.

They are twenty and twenty-one now. Number one son - the one who had wandered away from 'Doctor Who' - deals with spiders without much fuss, despite my earlier histrionics. That's pretty amazing I now feel.

Number two son doesn't scream - well, boys don't do they? - but he's very nervous around a spider.

And my husband? Well my poor, long-suffering husband is also nervous about spiders, 'though he can't admit it. I've never given him the opportunity. And it's taken me over twenty years to realise it.

I blithely assumed when we married that he would take over from my mother in rescuing me in spider crises. After all, no one in the world could be more frightened of them than me, could they?

Take, for example, that nature book that Auntie Vera gave me on my tenth birthday. It was a wonderful book. My favourite picture was a colour plate of pink cherry blossom in Kent, but I couldn't handle the book because another section held a quarter-page photograph of a spider with huge, bulbous belly.

When I was about sixteen I spent an entire evening sitting on top of our upright piano. My mother was out and a rampaging spider was scurrying between the settee in the middle of the room and the space beneath the bookcase - back and forth, all evening.

And to this day I'm careful how I handle tomatoes because of that leafy bit at the top that looks like a spider, especially when separated from the fruit.

So I took it for granted my husband was better disposed towards spiders than me. And indeed, he has always dealt with them for me.

It's his manner of dealing with them that rankles. I get cross with him for killing them instead of putting them outside. He tends to refer to medium-sized spiders as 'huge.' That in itself should have alerted me years ago to his real feelings towards them. And worst of all, I deplore his recent habit of vacuuming them up.

The vacuum technique was my idea actually. In the last year, with a truly huge spider at large, I would resort to the vacuum cleaner rather than abandon the room. But I hate doing it. Death by dust. How awful. See, I don't really think they're mean and menacing. Underneath that unfortunate exterior most spiders, I'm sure, are charming - except black widows of course, with their penchant for eating their husbands after mating - no, but on the whole, I've never doubted their friendly dispositions.

And suddenly there were two of us involved in the sadistic ritual of the vacuum cleaner. It was too much.

'I'll stop,' I said to my husband recently after a particularly ugly incident on the landing, 'if you will.'

And so it was agreed.

He probably thought I'd renege at the first crisis, but since then we've come through September and October - black months on any arachnophobics calender - and not a single intruder has been forced to bite the dust.

What then, you may ask, do I do instead?

Fellow arachnophobics won't believe this, but I'm getting over my fear. No honestly. I find I can deal with all specimens up to the size of, let's say, a pullets egg. Those in the 'huge' category are still a problem. But believe me, this is undreamed-of progress. A miracle, almost.

Only this morning number two son came across a large spider in the kitchen and I reached for a tea towel, picked the spider up and casually took him outside.

Number two son stood agog. Glorious moment.

I wish I could explain how it's come about. If I had a nice, neat answer to the problem I'd package it and patent it and probably make a fortune.

I can only say that it has something to do with my mounting guilt at watching an innocent spider meet a grisly death.

But beyond the guilt was the anger. Anger with my husband (poor man) that he couldn't pick them up in a duster. Anger that he should stamp on them, sometimes without killing them outright. Anger because he used the vacuum cleaner on them (never mind who's idea it was in the first place.) And anger with myself for being such a wimp.

'Damn it, I'll deal with it myself next time,' I said to him recently through gritted teeth as I looked down on yet another victim splayed and damp and lifeless on the kitchen floor.

And I really did. Number two son can confirm.

Now if I could just get angry about cruelty to slugs...

The Problem Patch

by

F C Trotter

The district social workers were delighted when the row of old cottages was demolished, the problem families rehoused in bright new council flats.

Developers cast speculative eyes at the site, the local councillors in their wisdom debated the merits of negotiated acquisition and compulsory purchase. But all the tentative plans formulated fell down for the same reason - there was no access. The rectangular site was shut in by a factory wall and a public footpath on its long sides, by the backs of houses and shops on its short ones.

So while men pondered problems they had themselves created, nature crept in to soften the harsh outlines of bared foundations and rubble remnants.

Grass and moss vied with abandoned garden plants for space. Coltsfoot spread gratefully from gardens where it had been long persecuted to burst into great patches of gold as each winter relaxed its grip. The first bird-brought seeds of willow-herb flourished, the pink spires gracing the midsummer days.

Men added their contribution in the form of dumped rubbish, some impermanent, capable of disintegration and absorption; some solid and long-lingering, tins, pans, old push-chairs and bikes.

Yet even these eyesores were quickly hidden as bramble grew thickly. An elderberry bush pushed its way up in the very centre of the site, a straggly sallow hid a crumbling wall with clusters of glowing catkins. Soon the site was almost inaccessible, crossed only by a few faint tracks made by the children who played there.

They appreciated the sanctuary of this miniature green oasis in a desert of brick and concrete. They sought the flowers which blossomed in Spring and Summer, the early Autumn blackberries. They watched the wildlife which shared the patch with them, wrens, robins and hedge sparrows in the brambles, itinerant goldfinches bobbing the seed-heads, butterflies basking in the sunshine.

Others saw it very differently. The owners must be made to tidy that overgrown site, said the council. So every year two old men would appear with bagging hooks and begin devastating the area, baring again the ugly metallic skeletons which were never removed.

All but the elder and sallow were levelled, the fallen remains gathered and cremated. Once a great fire was started with the elder as a centre-piece. When the men left that year it stood starkly bare, its limbs charred black. But the following Summer the creamy froth of its great flower heads hid most of the scars of its searing.

Now the problem of the patch has been resolved. Shops that back onto it and front the busy High Street have been sold. They will be pulled down and a big new store will take in most of the patch, a plan which is meeting with general approval.

But the children will miss their playground, like the birds they must go elsewhere. Others, as they walk along the footpath, will miss the greenness, the colours and scents of the seasons, the visions of the countryside condensed in those few square yards. And I shall no longer be able to step from the path and push my way through gossamer-hung brambles to gather bunches of plump, purple elderberries as I set out for a morning's fishing in the Autumn.

Dying for a Leak

by

Nigel Hemingford-Grey

I first met my hero, Charlie Wilson, at the local Church of England Primary School. St Barnabas was a good school although a bit old-fashioned. The classrooms were laid out in a regular pattern of double desks which were allocated alphabetically. Fate ordained that Watson and Wilson sat together and, for many years, we were inseparable.

Charlie had a generous sprinkling of freckles over his innocent face, a huge mop of ginger hair cut severely from the neck up to two protruding ears, and very dirty knees. Although his trousers appeared intact, his short-sleeved pullover was frayed round the bottom and one of his socks had a hole in the calf; this rarely showed, as their clearly ordained resting place was round his ankles. Shoes were 'serviceable' but had not seen polish since leaving the shop. My opening greeting of 'Hello' was returned with a casual 'ow do', but Charlie was more interested in the rest of the class, screwing his neck round to take in his new environment.

Our first teacher was Miss Rawnsley, pale and flat, with a soft penetrating voice. She immediately issued exercise books and pencils and got us to write something. Charlie's efforts were a few mis-shapen words and a pretty good likeness of a football match. This did not meet with approval, and started a war of attrition between Charlie and Miss Rawnsley that lasted the rest of our time at St Barnabas. It also revealed Charlie's left-handedness as there was an immediate clash of elbows on the crowded seat; we interchanged places, with Miss Rawnsley's obvious disapproval until we explained the reason.

Society uses many euphemisms, sometimes amusing, often indelicate, to indicate a visit to the toilet. As the headmaster rang the handbell for playtime, Charlie blurted out his version, 'dying for a leak', and shot out of the door before the crashing desk lid alerted Miss Rawnsley. I caught up with him later dangling his body upside-down from the solitary swing in the playground. From breathless bursts of conversation, I gathered that Charlie was the eldest of five children with his only sister, Eileen, the middle one. They lived in the Haworth Road Estate, three miles away across fields, which he always walked whatever the weather. He only missed school once, in the winter of 1933, when shoulder-high snow blanketed the countryside.

Alan Gibson got meningitis and died, but the rest of us went up to the intermediate class taught by Miss Cragg, a blonde top-heavy lady who pointed at us with her glasses. 'Craggy-pots' was an eccentric, much louder and faster than Miss Rawnsley. She could dash to the back of the class in a split second, and throw a piece of chalk with unerring precision. Nevertheless, she had a soft centre. There was one occasion when the headmaster had caught Charlie clambering onto the roof of the storehouse to retrieve a ball. It cost him 'six-of-the-best' and he spent the rest of the day rubbing his hands together to ease the pain. 'Craggy-pots' appeared to ignore the incident but, as she passed the suffering Charlie, a couple of toffees were quietly dropped onto his desk. Resentment changed to affection, and Charlie and I adored her from then on.

A second brush with authority arose over Charlie's sister, Eileen, who had now started at St Barnabas. One playtime she was being teased by the school bully, a big lad called Albert Jackson, who was dragging her around by her plaited hair. 'Gerroff ahr kid, Jacko!' shouted Charlie. 'You come and make me,' taunted Jacko, not releasing his hold. Charlie's face reddened. With slow deliberate strides he walked straight up to Eileen's tormentor, paused and crashed the clenched fist of his strong left arm into Jacko's nose. The bully collapsed in a squealing heap, whilst the playground erupted with high-pitched cheering. Charlie's inevitable visit to the headmaster was clearly *not* a painful experience, but he never told me what actually happened.

Our final time at St Barnabas was in Mr King's scholarship class. The seeds of knowledge so firmly planted by Miss Rawnsley and lovingly nurtured by 'Craggy-pots' were to be developed into prize-winning blooms under his direction, and the school proudly boasted an Honours board that proclaimed his successes. Whether it was spelling, grammar, arithmetic or nature, 'The King' had an instinctive ability to find your weaknesses. His tall, lean frame would suddenly bend over your desk, stab a finger into your mistake and gently mutter a correction. His quiet authority inspired confidence; he knew all the answers. During a painting lesson he discovered Charlie was colour-blind, and advised him how to cope with likely difficulties.

The scholarship papers finally arrived and were sympathetically handled by 'The King'. Nevertheless, nervous tension got to Charlie - 'dying for a leak' - and he had to be excused a couple of times. Eventually, after weeks of waiting, the results arrived. Charlie and I had both got through and were to start at the grammar school in September. Moreover, we had both gained scholarships, much to the relief of Charlie's Mum and Dad. We had our photographs taken by 'Craggy-pots' and, just before we left the school for good, we saw our names added in gold lettering to the Honours board.

The grammar school was a different world altogether, a frightening six-storey Victorian building of black, carved stone. For the first few weeks, Charlie and I frequently got lost, even from each other, as we looked little different from the other seven hundred boys in school uniform. As he was quite tall by now, Charlie's Mum and Dad had started him off in long trousers, so the familiar grubby knees disappeared for good except for sports and gym.

He developed into a good gymnast - in his element leaping from springboards or twining himself round ropes and wall-bars. Unfortunately, the school did not cater for Charlie's abiding passion, soccer, so he had to make do with Rugby football. He didn't really bother with the laws or principles of the game, but enthusiasm was outstanding; his performances were always interrupted by a string of penalties for offside or over-robust play.

Our academic progress rested exclusively in the hands of male staff clad in gowns. The only ladies we encountered served out the dinners, except for the headmaster's secretary, a scared little rabbit who rarely braved the teaching arena. Four years ahead lay School Certificate, but the first year was spent in discovering our natural talents. Neither Charlie nor I were any great shakes at Latin or Greek, so we gradually ploughed our way up the 'modern' side of the curriculum, increasingly showing ability in the sciences. Charlie's speciality was chemistry, whilst mine was maths; physics occupied an intermediate position. Consequently, many evenings of science homework proved to be a combined effort, with Charlie's trusty bicycle providing essential transport.

The aftermath of School Certificate saw the first hint of separation between Charlie and me. In the sixth forms, maths and science tended to conduct their own specialist classes, and for the first time since meeting my old stable-mate we no longer shared all our classes. Whilst he threatened the fabric of the buildings during chemistry practicals, I wrestled with integral calculus. Our final parting came with successful attempts at Higher School Certificate, and recruitment for the war in Europe.

I was allowed to go to university to study for a shortened degree in physics, followed by posting to a radar station near Lands End - to watch and wait. Typically, Charlie went straight into the Royal Artillery, invaded France on D-day plus two and, as he put it, 'did a spot of liberating'. We corresponded during this traumatic period, and I still treasure some of his vivid mud-stained letters: 'Sorry about the mess; we're stuck in a slit trench under mortar attack.'

At the end of hostilities, I returned to university, read mathematics and went into banking. Charlie was less fortunate. His Mum and Dad could not afford to send him to university, because of their concern for his younger brothers and sister. He got a job at the local dyeworks, but studied for his Higher National Certificate part-time at the technical college. We were now hundreds of miles apart and our correspondence had become a mere trickle; ultimately, it was a few terse comments in the annual Christmas card. He moved to Lincolnshire in 1964 to join a new company manufacturing Nylon.

Ten years later, I was horrified to learn of the terrible explosion at Flixborough and to read the name of Charles Alfred Wilson amongst the twenty eight fatal casualties. The Court of Inquiry established the cause of the accident as a leak in a hydrocarbon feed-pipe. The Scunthorpe Coroner returned verdicts of Accidental Death, but I know the whimsical turn of phrase Charlie would have used!

The Apple Orchard

by

Tony Bridge

To my child's eye the old farmhouse was a mansion, full of mysterious dark nooks and endless hiding places. It was no longer the hub of farm activity; most of the land had been sold off years before, but it was always full of people visiting the old farmer's friendly widow. She loved company, and her house was always open. I grew up in that house. My mother died when I was five, and I was taken in by the old widow and brought up as her own, sharing her love with Sarah, her daughter. Sarah was angelic, the epitome of beauty and generosity. We talked endlessly as we sat beside the pond in the orchard, munching on crisp, fleshy apples. We said that we would never part from each other, and spent the warm hazy days of the Kentish summers daydreaming of our life together in a cottage amid the hop-fields and oasthouses. Such are childhood dreams. We had both attended the local school, but the time to leave soon came. Sarah had always been clever, and was to go to grammar school in the nearby town. We were to be separated after all. That last summer was bitter sweet, and so very short. After years together, I felt a part of my own body was being torn off.

Life set into a new routine. I attended the local secondary school and helped the widow whenever I could. I saw Sarah at weekends, but she was growing up fast. She became more interested in her friends from school and the town. We began to grow apart, but when I said as much, she quickly rebuked me, insisting she still loved me, and would never forget our childhood. The years passed quickly. I finished school as soon as I could and started work for the widow, managing the orchard. Sarah was living in town with a friend. I had not seen her for a while, until one day. It was a Saturday, in mid-July. The weather was exceptionally hot. It had not rained for months, and the ground was cracking. The farmers were worried about their crops. Even the hops were withering. I was idle, and lonely. I had no interests outside the farm. My work, the widow, and most of all Sarah: those were the only things important to me.

It was in this melancholy mood that I wandered past the house. The ivy-clad walls no longer offered me comfort and protection. The gloom behind the windows merely echoed the gloom in my heart. Suddenly, however, my heart jumped. I had heard the voice that always lightened my mood. It was Sarah. She sounded as bubbly as ever, and her words danced through my brain like butterflies through the apple blossom. I ran in, wanting only to throw my arms around her and never let go. Through the blackness of my sun-blinded vision, I could make out the shape of the widow, and then my darling Sarah, and then, another figure, a tall, well-built man, who held Sarah's hand in his own. I stopped, my mind racing. I looked again, praying that it was an illusion. Then Sarah saw me. Her eyes lit up and she threw her arms round me. I was confused. Then she confirmed what I had already guessed.

'John, I'd like you to meet Charles, we're going to be married!' She grinned eagerly. He held out his hand in friendly welcome. I shook it roughly, mumbled how glad I was for them, made the excuse of being on an errand and went out. I ran across the fields, until I felt faint. My world had fallen apart. I could not return to the farmhouse. I could not face that look of tenderness on Sarah's face, that was directed not at me, but at him.

Sarah was married a week later. I could not face going, so I feigned illness. The widow guessed the truth however, and said she understood. This did little to cheer me up. I turned my efforts to work, desperate to block out the pain. The seasons quickly turned, with all the work they involved in the orchard, and I was soon facing another summer. This year was hotter and dryer than the last, and the trees started dying in the orchard. I knew how they felt. The heat seemed to sap all the life from me, and the sun stared mockingly down. Summer had always been my favourite season when I was young. Now, it left me thinking of Sarah. I would sit, day after day, by the green mud that had been the pond and dream about our childhood days. As I sat and stared, I saw myself in that pond, sterile, dank and decaying.

With seemingly all nature giving up life that summer, it was no surprise that the widow was taken ill. One day, I was called from the fields. She had asked for me. Her eyes smiled as I sat beside her bed and took her hand. She told me that she was worried about her daughter, that she had not wanted her to marry Charles. I tried to quieten her, but to no avail. Suddenly pain spread across her face and her breathing grew faint. 'Look after Sarah, she needs you', she said, and fell silent. Her hand grew limp in mine, and I knew the person who had guided me for so long had gone.

I moved out of the farmhouse after her funeral, to the cottage where I was born, at the other end of the orchard. Two weeks later Sarah and her husband moved in. I would see her occasionally, by the pond, eating an apple, and ask her how she was. She always said things were fine, but I could see sadness in her eyes, a sadness that made my heart bleed for her. I began to hear rumours about Charles in the village. He would spend the day in the inn, downing mugs of beer and gambling with the labourers. There was also talk of him mucking about with some of the local girls. Sarah must have known these stories, indeed I often heard raised voices from the farmhouse when Charles decided to go home. However, though I longed to help her, I knew I ought not to interfere.

Then one day, later that summer, I was in the pub at the same time as Charles. I fought hard to stay calm as he boasted of how he had slept with a farmer's two daughters the day before. I thought only of the look in Sarah's eyes, as I walked to the nearby town. I saw Charles again on my way home. He had just left the pub and could hardly stand. I followed as he staggered home. I watched him go into the farmhouse, and it was not long before I heard the usual raised voices. This time however, there was more violence in his words. Suddenly I heard a punch landing, and Sarah screamed out in pain. Again a punch. He was hitting her. I could take no more. Anger welled up in my body. I burst in, and wrestled Charles to the ground. I felt his fist pound into my face, and was overwhelmed by the alcohol on his breath. He struck at me again, this time landing a punch in my stomach. I struggled to breathe, the world span, and everything started to grow dim. Then I heard him strike at Sarah again. I could hear her begging him to stop between the sobs that almost choked her. This cleared my head and I struggled to my feet. I caught Charles by surprise with a punch in the kidneys, he doubled up and I hit him again, this time with all the might that my uncontrollable anger could produce. He stumbled backwards, lost his footing and crashed to the floor. The crunch of his skull smashing against the solid oak table filled the room. I blacked out.

It could only have been seconds, but it seemed like hours later that I came to. There was a pool of blood beside Charles' head. His eyes stared blankly back at me. I shuddered. I looked around, Sarah was gone. I rushed outside, not noticing that the sky was filled with angry clouds, and the noise of the birds was drowned by the crashing of thunder. I ignored the rain lashing against my face. I just ran, calling her name at the top of my voice, as the lightning flashed overhead. I could not see her, but I kept running. Then I tripped. I hit the ground and the world grew dark.

They found her body a day later, lying in the mud and rotting leaves by the edge of the pond, her eyes staring searchingly into the water, her hand pressing a single, rotten apple against her heart.

Revenge

by

K L Baseden

The clock struck nine and she awoke with a start, rattling the cup in its saucer still resting on her lap. She steadied it with a fragile, hand, and was still for a few seconds taking in her surroundings. All was quiet. She breathed a relaxed even breath. Time for another hot drink before bed, she thought. Taking the packet of milk from the fridge, she shook it a little. Just enough for one drink. It meant a long walk to the village shop in the morning, but it was worth it. No milk deliveries meant no empties, no doorstep ammunition, for 'them'.

There had been peace for almost three days. No shouts and taunts. One night while she leant her body against the front door pleading with them to leave her alone, hands thrust through the letterbox grabbing at her. Foul, abusive language invaded her ears and she was paralysed with fear. Finally after what seemed like hours they had left, only to return many times over the past weeks. The night held its own fear. She tried to sleep, but daylight was her only sanctuary. There were times while in the village she had almost told someone, but a greater fear prevented it. Fear of the consequences.

Suddenly her train of thought was interrupted by the milk threatening to boil over. She quickly turned off the gas and reached for her mug but stopped abruptly, her arms remaining outstretched, she listened hard. 'Please don't let it be', she thought aloud. Voices mingled, muffled by the night air they rose and diminished. Her eyes focused intently on the front door. Just passers-by after all? Encouraged she half turned back to the kitchen.

'Have you missed us?'

The voice was mocking. She dared to look towards the letterbox, where all she could see were hideous wriggling fingers threatening to reach her, envelope her in their grip.

'We are tired of waiting. We will be back for you soon, very soon!'

She wasn't aware of the silence for a few minutes. They had gone - for now. It was important to work fast. She remembered seeing a small tub of putty under the sink. It had been there since her late husband had repaired a pane of glass in the kitchen. She went to the bathroom cabinet and searched it frantically. Yes there were some left! She worked a little of the putty between her stiff fingers. It was fiddly, but she managed to line the inside of the letterbox. The next part proved even trickier. Her concentration was intense. Her heartbeat echoed in her ears. Twice she nicked her fingers, but quickly sucked the drops of blood and carried on. Finally she carefully dropped the flap that concealed the neatly positioned razor blades.

Returning purposefully to the kitchen she lit the gas, re-heated the milk and made her drink - at last. Then she went calmly to her armchair, adjusted the cushions, took a sip of hot chocolate, and settled back to wait.

The Ride to Alice

by

Julie Lynn

I am one of the few people who has visited Alice Springs and not made it to Ayers Rock. I am not proud of this. It is a strange thing to have to say and it isolates me. There is even the hint of something a little chaotic.

But no worries. Because Alice Springs is a strange and isolating town. And when I got there, in April 1988, it was also in a state of chaos.

The ride to Alice had started two days before, at a Brisbane bus station, where an erratic sky teased tempers and cardigans. There I settled in preparation for a trip into the unknown. And that's where I went.

The nowhere that lay inside Queensland was red and dusty and dangerous. 'Fuck off or you're dead' was what it said to visitors. It had two road-houses, the first of which was 'Augathella'. Here, during darkness, I sipped tea outside a shack and listened to an unintelligible Dutch woman who claimed to be eighty-two and on her way home to 'Darvin'.

Later, after night had thinned to an unnecessarily bright early morning, the coach stopped again. This time the road-house swam with the smell of fried eggs and offered a spartan, lonely dining area. Most of us stood outside to chew our bacon sandwiches or lamingtons or swig from cans. Others, meanwhile, yawned, stretched their legs and stepped tentatively on the hot, cracked ground, scratching their heads and taking photos of what was beyond both focus and comprehension.

When we pulled away, I was startled to realise that Winton was indeed a place of human habitation. Shacks across the road, the fraying edge of some remote outback settlement, may have been shacks, but they were also homes. On one verandah an old tennis racket lay beside a ball. Nearby, a band of Aboriginals, mostly in their mid-adolescence plus one small one at the back, roamed and scuffed and trotted. Feet, knees, girls' dresses betrayed to travellers that here was truly a dry and dusty place. A place with no bathrooms, I thought miserably, shifting my shoulders and wondering when next I would be able to wash my hair.

For two dollars I hired a towel, shampoo and soap and took a shower at a hotel in Mount Isa. The drink afterwards in the bar was one of the best of my continental grand tour, because I wasn't fantasizing about having a hot shower, regaining some privacy and forgetting that I was a traveller. Instead, I had a chat with a civil servant from Essex and an audio-typist from Surfer's Paradise.

Mount Isa was ninety-six degrees and a wide main road was the spine along which long cars, utes and combies cruised, as if there were nowhere to drive to from Mount Isa. Which there wasn't. All I needed to know about this mining town was that it was en route to the Red Centre. The heart. My precious, my very own, ride to Alice.

Off again and night gathered swiftly. Soon it appeared we'd forsaken not only light, but Order - motels, telephones, a decent road, safety... here the track stabbed viciously at the tyres, the underbelly of the coach, and dragged us crazily into and out of pot-holes the size of a small ditch. Then something strange happened. It began to rain. At first it was just big soft drops, a gentle, reassuring rhythm to counter the battle beneath us. Gradually though it got fast and angry and remained so until we reached Tenant Creek, some tapes, some conversations, some discomfort later. There everybody dashed damply into a carpeted reception room in a building that may have been all there was to Tenant Creek. More tea, more talk. All gathering against a collective sleep deficit. No doubt there would be tears before bedtime. But bedtime never came. Oblivion surfaced only briefly, delicately, in little waves that swept you, minutes later, on to some waking shore where once more you wondered if you'd slept. Stranded, you could only look out of the window and into the undreamable beyond. The dreamtime.

What was beyond, beyond the times of our wildest dreams, was an infinity of orange sludge. This was what you got when rain hammered a red desert, when it gave the dust what for. Scrub was the only sign that water here meant life. But here was trauma. The sodden desert with a black sky shedding its hefty black water holds fewest options, is not one to get hopeful about. I determined to remember this next time I sat in a surburban kitchen, a bowl of flowers before me, and reflected gloomily on the prospects for a very rainy day.

It couldn't last though. The rain couldn't get any more ferocious, not here, not in the Middle where it was supposed to be dry and parched. Not in a town like Alice. Alice Springs: was it really a place? Or was it just folklore like London, Paris, New York...? I looked out of the window and I looked forward to Arrival, to Getting There. The tedium and hopelessness of the drenched landscape made me crave the heat, the flies, the notoriety of hot places. I switched on my Walkman and listened to The Warumpi Band (Big Name No Blankets), courtesy of a fellow traveller. The orange sludge continued.

First impressions of Alice Springs were demoralising. My expectations of the extraordinary were entirely thwarted. For a start it was still grey, thumping with water, reminding me of a place I'd been before. Another factor was the terrible ordinariness of the view: a breaker's yard, a building supplies yard - the quasi-industrial backside of any modern settlement. Like some approach to Plymouth or Wigan. The sort of thing you saw from train windows as you rushed past small towns.

The weather could do what it liked, but it couldn't dampen the splendour of the shopping centre, with its tinkling fountains, rockeries, its glass wizardry, the flashiest escalator in the southern hemisphere. I browsed in the bookshop, waiting for the rain to ease, and bought The Man Who Mistook His Wife For A Hat, which is a book about chaos.

Minutes later I'm witnessing a fight. This is more like it. A short and thin drunken Aboriginal man lunges at a large Aboriginal woman and snatches something, maybe a twenty dollar note. He attempts to nip away, but nipping anywhere is sadly beyond him. The woman lets out a great roar, leaps after him on surprisingly thin legs and fetches him an almighty blow to the skull. She is furious - no doubt about this at all. The little brown Stan Laurel is knocked flying into a goalkeeper's dive, but he saves nothing. And it's not funny. The woman shouts and wallops him as he lies on the paved precinct, clasping his head, and rocking and sobbing into the now-slow rain.

All day the rain stops and starts and keeps the feet of all the Aborigines wet. But around six the sky over the middle of Australia shatters beneath all the world's water. Eleven inches between then and when I woke early the following morning, woken again by the drum roll of water. This was not on, not in Alice Springs. I'd finished reading all the tales of madness and disorder in The Man Who Mistook His Wife For A Hat. So I lay and stared out of the window at a telephone kiosk in which water was rising like a test tube under a tap.

A lot of feet had got wet, and some had got washed away. Nine Aborigines, dreaming on the bed of the usually dry Todd River lost their lives when the river gave up its dust and became a river again. I knew it was true because overhead there were Channel Seven helicopters...

Yes, the river bubbled happily, as if it had discovered an appetite for water. There was another appetite, too. Near the far bank a black woman sat in the arms of a tree, inches from death and the promise of chaos. And another dreamtime.

I never did get to Ayers Rock. There was no access through the flooded Simpson Gap. And I was tired. Part of the journey plan meant not getting there, I decided: Not Arriving. It was about coping with chaos and a resolve to return.

I washed some underwear at the launderette and two days later headed north for Darwin.

The Eagle Has Landed

by

Stephen Passey

The starcraft landed, making no sound in the null-atmosphere of the dusty world. Fully-adjustable stabilizer legs slid out of their containing pods and connected with the ground, causing little puffs of dust-clouds to rise up from the surface of the planetoid. The stabilizers aligned themselves to the uneven terrain, sinking about seven inches into the grey, sandy dust. For about a minute, the craft was inactive. Then, from a tube positioned in the huge bows of the ship, a small probe was fired with great speed across the surface.

As the probe returned its data into the Central Processor of the starship Saracen, Commander Tryan observed the surface scans on the relay screen.

'The planetoid appears to be totally devoid of all life, commander,' an officer addressed the stern figure. 'No plants, not even algae, not surprising with the air content it has. It's just a dead rock, sir. Why can't we turn back now?'

The commander gave the young man a sharp eye. 'Our mission is to retrace the birth planets, Serrak, not to retreat in the face of a few failures.'

'But sir, this is just a stranded planetoid, it doesn't even have an orbital path - a lump of useless rock strewn off of some distant planet.'

The murmurs in the command room were now far too evident to Tryan. The crew were light-years from home. If he could just keep them a little longer...

'Send a ground party, you, Serrak, Goyran, Alders and I shall investigate the surface. Man the restructurers to send us down, Lieutenant Lyanders, please.'

The group of four trooped military-style into the suit room. They each took one of the light, metallic life-suits and zipped themselves into the protective layers of material. Tryan picked up one of the stun phasers and slipped it into his pocket without the other three noticing.

'Oh,' he remarked, 'we won't be needing any weapons, Serrak,'

The party walked swiftly into the restructuring pod. It was a large, circular room, with clean, smooth and undetailed walls that belied it's complexity.

'Prepare to destructure, commander,' Lyanders voice came clear over the communicators.

'Destructuring, now...'

Commander Tryan's body began to evaporate into separate particles in a shimmering cloak of light. The other crewmembers were also dissipating with speed. A wash of light swept across the room, recording exactly all the information needed to restructure the team.

On the surface of the dead world, a patch of light appeared. Four crewmembers of the Imperial Starship Saracen were restructured about thirty metres from where the great colossus was sitting on its titanium support pods.

Tryan looked around the dusty vista that came to his eyes. They were close to something of a great importance, he knew, but when would it come? When would he find the birth worlds? And could, would his crew be patient until then?

'Commander, let us start the exploration,' the scientist Goyran spoke over the close-range communicator.

'Why don't we start over at the ridge,' Alders suggested rather snidely.

The four found it easy to move about on the planetoid's surface. The gravitational pull was estimated at a sixth of their home planet Aurelia's pull. Within an hour they had reached the ridge.

'That should be far enough,' said Serrak.

'Far enough for what?' Tryan began to look about worriedly. His left hand fumbled in his servo pocket for the phaser.

Serrak saw the commander's phaser rise up towards him. With lightening-quick actions, he drew his own lasgun and fired wildly in the commander's direction. The commander took a hit in the leg, spun on one foot and, his gun firing uselessly into the airless void, he tripped on a jutting piece of rock and collapsed.

Serrak fired three more shots into the motionless body, replaced his weapon and radioed back to the ship.

'This is Serrak, the commander has been killed in an accident, we must leave for home as soon as possible, it is too dangerous to remain here.'

Smiling, the three crewmembers returned to their ship. As Serrak plotted a new course, back to Aurelia, he turned to Goyran.

'Did you actually ever believe any of that man's theories, that any of the birth worlds, where our race was founded, still exist?'

'I had always believed,' said the officer, 'that the worlds of the first era were evaporated in the Great Wars.'

A murmur went about the crew, some of them didn't even believe that the Great Wars had ever occurred.

'It was only a thought,' said Serrak, 'prepare to fire primary thrusters...'

As the starship Saracen zoomed at high speed off the surface of the barren world, the commander's body rolled off of the rocky spike it was lying over. Yet the commander had not tripped on rock, for, half buried by dust and half worn by micrometeor showers was a steel landing gear. The dust shifted a little as the planetoid began to move into the outer regions of a nebula of gas. As it fell back to reveal the metal underneath, the starship was a mere spot of light in the sky.

Written, in a form of language too ancient for any of the modern human race to understand, were three words.
APOLLO 11, NASA
Maybe the commander had found the remaining of the birth worlds after all...

Emptiness

by

Roger Davis

She was always there, every evening on his way home. He saw her and she took his breath away. On a crowded railway platform she quite simply stood out, a gay, delightfully wistful woman, with long blonde hair and sparkling blue eyes. Obviously, an experienced commuter, she always stood in the same place and when the train arrived she was in exactly the right position to step elegantly aboard.

For many weeks he saw her and his pulse raced as he approached the platform and walked along towards her. She smiled, was it at him? In the scramble to get aboard, they never actually sat together, but across the carriage there was an undeniable empathy between them.

She got off the train two stations before he did. She smiled as she slammed the door shut - but still no words.

He too got off the train at her station. He followed her along the platform, out of the station and along the leafy avenue. He fell in step with her and their hands touched and held. They strolled slowly along, a slight drizzle was beginning to fall, but they hardly noticed it.

'Do you know where you are going?' she asked.

'No, I don't really care,' he answered.

She paused and turned to face him. 'You are too honest.' She stood on tiptoe and kissed him gently on the lips - it was like a physical attack on him.

'I've been waiting so long to kiss you,' she whispered.

'Me too!' he said, breathlessly.

The drizzle had turned into rain; the car tyres sang as they drove along the wet road, but still they walked slowly along the avenue.

Suddenly, she stopped, a large white gate and a grand drive led through a lawn to a Georgian house.

'I live here,' she said, looking up at him. She touched his cheek, 'with my parents.'

He tenderly wiped away a raindrop from her forehead. 'I am so glad to have met you,' he said. 'Let us sit together on the train tomorrow and talk. I want to know everything about you.'

'Yes, I'd like that,' she replied, 'I can't wait for tomorrow.'

He let go of her hand and turned away from her and skipped around the puddles which were forming on the wet pavement.

The following evening he walked along the street towards the station, not seeming to notice the rain or the other people. It was no use hurrying, the train had long since gone.

Thankfully, it had been a busy day at the office, but how he longed for six o'clock when he normally left for the train.

At four o'clock he sat back in his chair and closed his eyes. He could see her standing next to him; they were chatting together and he felt so comfortable, so easy being with her.

The telephone on his desk rang; he slowly and reluctantly opened his eyes, not wanting the image to fade. He answered on the sixth ring. It was the Chairmans secretary, the Chairman would like to see him in the boardroom at four thirty.

His heart sank, these meetings tended to go on and on. The chances of getting to the station on time were indeed remote.

He was right, the meeting did go on and as he walked across the station concourse towards the platform the time was almost seven o'clock.

The platform was less crowded at this time. Would she be there, at the same place, waiting for him?

The particular spot was deserted but commuters gradually surrounded him as the train arrived.

He sat next to the window, it was dark now and raining even heavier. He stared out of the window but could only see the reflection of the seats being occupied. Then he saw - he turned quickly towards the seat opposite, but it was empty, as empty as he felt inside.

In the Beginning

by

A H Addis

In the beginning, God created the heaven and the earth. And the earth was without form and void; and darkness was upon the face of the deep. And God did not know what to do next, so he sat down and created thinking. And as he was deep in thought, he was suddenly aware of someone beside him.

'Who is there?' God asked (because he could not see, since everything was black).

'I'm Man,' came the reply. 'I come from the future - you see, I have perfected time travel. You must be just starting the creation: don't let me disturb you.'

So the Lord thought for a moment and then he said, 'Let there be light!' And behold, there was light. And God divided the light from the darkness. And he called the light Day; and the darkness he called Night. And God saw that it was good.

But Man said, ' You can't have twelve hours of darkness and twelve hours of daylight, just like that.' And he explained to God about Greenwich Mean Time, and British Summer Time, and the International Date Line, and how (if you travel in a certain direction) you can reach your destination the day before you have even left your point of departure. And then he explained how there are sixty seconds in every minute, and sixty minutes in every hour, and twenty-four hours in every day, and thirty-one days in every month (but sometimes there are thirty, or occasionally twenty-eight or nine), and three hundred-and-sixty-five days in every year (except when there are three-hundred-and-sixty-six), until the Lord grew terribly confused indeed, and wondered if it was that good after all. (But he carried on with the Creation, just the same.)

And on the second day, God said, 'Let there be a firmament, and let it divide the heaven from the earth.' And it was so. And God saw that it was good.

But Man said, 'Oh, it's not like that anymore.' And he explained to God about global warming, and the ozone layer, and the greenhouse effect, and how he had destroyed the earth's atmosphere by using aerosol cans and dangerous chemicals, until the Lord grew rather displeased. And he saw that it was not good. (But he carried on with the Creation, just the same.)

And on the third day, God said, 'Let the waters be gathered together in one place, and let the dry land appear.' And it was so. And God called the dry land Earth; and the gathering together of the waters he called Seas.

And God said, 'Let the earth bring forth grass, the herb yielding seed, and the fruit tree yielding fruit after its kind.' And it was so, and the Lord saw that it was good.

But Man said, 'Oh, these no longer exist.' And Man explained to God how he had plundered the land, and felled the great forests, polluted the crops and laid waste to the vegetation in the many wars he had fought. And God grew very angry indeed, but he still carried on with the Creation.

And on the fourth day, God said, 'Let there be lights in the firmament.' And he made the warm sun, and the moon, and he made the stars also. And God saw that it was good.

But Man said, 'These are not the same either.' And Man explained to God how he had found a way of reaching the stars and had exhausted their mineral supplies, and destroyed their forms of life, and how he had drained the energy from the sun so that now it was dying, and how all the other planets were cold and dead, and the earth was a cold place too. And God saw that it was not good at all and he was filled with despair. Yet still he carried on with the Creation.

And on the fifth day, God said, 'Let the waters bring forth living creatures, and let there be fowl that fly in the air, and beasts that may creep upon the earth.' And it was so. And the Lord saw that it was good.

But Man shook his head. 'Nor do these still live,' he said. And Man explained to God how he had contaminated the water and the air with filthy slicks and clouds of poisonous gas, and how all the living creatures on the earth had died and none was left, until the Lord grew very sad. And he saw that it was bad, and he was loath to carry on with the Creation.

And on the sixth day, Man said to God, 'This is the day when you create me in your image, after your likeness; and you let me have dominion over the whole earth and all its living creatures, that I may rule over them.'

But God looked around the barren and desolate wasteland in the dying embers of civilisation, and he saw that it was not good.

And Man hung his head in shame and said, 'I'm sorry, Lord.'

And God said, 'So am I.'

The Washing Up

by

Helen Fairfield

This is not a subject which is likely to hit the headlines unless of course suicide was the result of having too much of it around. A pre-disposing factor not often brought to light in court cases but nevertheless worthy of consideration in the future perhaps. On the other hand, more enlightened folk might consider themselves fortunate to have enough food to make the plates, dishes, pans and cutlery dirty, considering that so much of the world's population have little or no washing up to do; not an enviable situation either. So where do we stand as regards this three times a day pile up? In front of the sink, no doubt, with the radio on in an effort to relieve the monotony.

But there are moments when these things are not all hum-drum. For example, on one occasion I was attempting to raise my thoughts above the level of the task in hand when there was an explosion in a kitchen cupboard. A dark brown ooze spread slowly and snake-like across the pristine freshness of the white thermo-plastic tiles. Bravely opening the cupboard door, with not a soul to witness my courage, I discovered a burst tin of prunes. I immediately put pen to paper and wrote to the manufacturers and suggested that if this sort of thing was their general policy at the canning factory, could they please supply me with a tin of exploding custard to accompany it.

The reply I received was a dissertation on the chemical factors involved on the subject of exploding prunes and enclosed was a postal order for sixty pence. This I thought showed integrity if not humour. But I think everyone will agree that this small incident did something to enliven the domestic chore.

But I would like to relate another experience of which I heard tell. An elderly friend had achieved her seventieth year and at intervals throughout her special day friends and relations had called bringing good wishes and gifts. In return they had all indulged in drinks and snacks. At the end of the day her kitchen bore witness to her hospitality and out came the pinafore and rubber gloves. The warmth of the water on her hands reminded her of the first time she had been allowed to wash up, standing on a chair with a vast apron tied round her. Her thoughts moved on to her children and grandchildren who had done the same thing. She almost heard the shrieks of delight as they endlessly washed the milk bottles and spoons. She had always ignored the pools on the floor. They were happily occupied and while doing that they were not doing anything worse. She could almost see their tiny round hands with dimples on the back so unlike her own ageing joints and blue veins visible under her thinning skin.

As she washed the small plates she remembered the children's parties with sausages and crisps piled high, and the time when the next door child had left the games and whispered in her ear to ask if she could have another grass sandwich. She had never seen mustard and cress before.

She dismissed from her mind the memories of the broken china, the result of adolescent carelessness and truculence and felt relieved that this was all finished long ago, though at the moment it all seemed very near. She could not recall the difficulties of her own growing up years, only the fun when she and her friends, when the boys suggested it, had formed a line right down the length of the kitchen and dining room and the dried up articles had been thrown from one to another down the line and finally put away in the proper places. Nothing had been broken; except a few teen-age hearts perhaps. She wondered where they all were now.

She changed the washing up water and started on the glasses stacked on a tray behind her, when a brutal sadness infiltrated her mind. Her hands worked more and more slowly. Her late husband had always washed the glasses when there had been extra to do and the thought of it became intolerable. She was now aware of her extreme tiredness. She stretched out her hand for the drying up cloth on the radiator but she felt not linen but warm, rough tweed. She heard his quiet voice as if speaking from far away.

'I'm waiting for you,' he said. 'You don't have to do all that by yourself.'

A Fare Terminated

by

Caroline Sumnall

'Ow soon?' she spoke with a disgruntled tone.
'November, early November.' Less than a month.
'Our John, you dunna know what this means. The house. The kids. Our lives. Everything will change. I'm a local girl John, local born and bred. You canna expect us to move and South? We anna a part of that. We dunna belong.'
Even as she spoke, her face lined with worry, unable to shout or cry, he knew that she would go. She had promised to honour and love him. She had vowed to obey.
'Alright John? You looked well gone for a second back then, ain't gonna catch that train if you don't get a move on, mate.'
'Aye, thanks, just thinking, you know, I was just taking a last decka at the place.'
Strange, he thought. It was the first time since he had arrived that he had slipped back into Northern tongue. Although his wife had remained exactly the same, working in the city and living in the suburbs had changed him. Now the Staffordshire man inside him was returning. It recognised that he was going home.
'Good luck to yer son - ain't gonna be the same no more without you runnin' in 'ere every night. Anyway I'd better get on, papers ain't gonna sell 'emselves. See yer round, mate.'
'Aye, Dave, look after yourself.'
He took a last look around the place. He remembered when he had first entered, three years ago last November. He had bought a paper and received a smile with it. Dave Cassey, his first friend in London. Quite a bargain for thirty two pence......
The tannoy interrupted his train of thought. He glanced at his watch. Damm! 5.13pm. Two minutes.
He ran down the platform with his tie flying behind him as the guard blew the whistle. Late again and he had been determined not to be. He hurriedly boarded and listened to the grunts as the commuters moved up to accommodate his slim frame. He put his suitcase on the rack above him and rested.

He gazed out of the window, amazed at the little details he had never noticed before; The dry, grey gum trodden into the tarmac; The corroding iron girders above; The obscenities written on the waiting room door. All had been strangely overlooked, although he had stared their way many times before. He had observed, but never really taken it all in. He felt like someone who was about to move house. It was too late to reconsider, but somehow he was compelled to stay, unable to close the door on this part of his life. The guard in his neatly pressed British Rail uniform forced him out with a whistle.

As the train pulled away from the station he told himself not to be so stupid, it was all for the best. He turned his head and gazed into the endless black tunnel embarrassed at his sentimentality. He had no need to be. Everyone was either reading the 'Evening Standard' or they were asleep. Commuters never noticed anything, except noise that is, which is silently forbidden. They are a race of their own, just speechless travellers.

It was the last time he would go to the office, the last time he would see her face. It had been the perfect relationship. He had had it all. At home he had his wife and kids, Karen now five and Tom almost ten and then at work she had always been there. Forever by his side.

It had been three years since their relationship had begun. Three long years, but he wished that they had been longer and he wanted to stay. He had seen her the day he had arrived at the company. He was the new manager with her as his assistant. It was a promotion and he had brought the family down to London in order to take up the position. He remembered how pleased he had been, but how his wife's expression portrayed her emotions clearly. Initially she complained, but as much as they loved where they lived, his family realised how important the position was to him and supported his decision to leave. Now it had all gone sour. She had got in the way and his wife had given him an ultimatum. He could either have her or his family, but not both. He had made his decision, it had been easy, it had been made the day Tom was born. He had come from a broken home and was determined not to put his kids through the trauma which had been forced on him. He knew where his priorities lay. That is not to say that he wanted to leave. The emotions welling inside him portrayed this clearly, but he knew what he had chosen to do was right.

They were moving back up North at the end of the week and they would be living close to her parents, just like before, in exactly the same district almost as if nothing had changed, but it definitely had. Even if his wife could erase the past three years he could not. He had formed a relationship he would never forget. It had meant so much to him. They had been the best years of his life.

Now he would no longer have all the responsibility and status of being a manager and letting go really hurt. Still, he had known that when he had made his decision and for better or for worse he would return.

The train slowed and drew into London Bridge with an abrupt halt. The passengers boarded, obviously weary from their individual troubles and strife which had occurred throughout the day. No one spoke. He would not miss his journey. It always made him smile though, the way the commuters never said a word. Antisocial to the end. He had never really got used to that. In the North it was all so friendly. Everyone knew everything about each other, just plain nosey he guessed, but at least they were never silent. No, that was definitely not a word you could possibly use to describe a Northerner. He broke the silence with a chuckle; someone looked up from their paper and glared. It was just not done. He knew the rules, or should do. He had been going home from London on the 5.15pm for three years and there had never been so much as a hello. Strange, he knew the lines on those faces intimately, but he did not even know their names.

He looked once again to the window as his neighbour turned to the sports pages. The only other noise was the guard's whistle as the train pulled out from the platform. The last stretch of the journey. The last time he would have to do it. No regrets. Only another hour and he would be home. Back to his wife and kids. His priorities. His choice.

As he gazed into the dark sky and looked at the stars, he remembered what he had done only an hour before and he drifted off the rails back into the office.

Everyone else was leaving, to give them plenty of time to catch the five o'clock. They would never get away with it anywhere else, but the company was fairly lenient about leaving times. As the lights in other rooms were switched off one by one, he looked around his room sipping his near - cold coffee, which as every manager knows is a vital piece of equipment. He would miss this place. Every last inch of it from the pictures on the wall to the carpet on the floor, both of which he had grown attached to. He looked at the photographs of his wife and children on his desk and smiled to himself as he remembered how long it had taken to get Karen to stand still for that shot.

This room was filled with memories and had become a part of him. Even the ghastly lime green wallpaper which had been under threat of removal every day since he had arrived, was now something he would gladly suffer. If only he could remain here, slumped in his comfortable worn leather armchair forever.

Life would have been perfect if she hadn't interfered. At that moment he wanted to pull her to pieces, but he knew he could never do anything like that to her, she was far too valuable. Like the rest of the room she was a part of the furniture, a fixed indentation on his brain. A part of him. A part he would never forget. A part he loved in a way he could not explain. No one would ever understand.

It was the nights he had stayed over working which had annoyed his wife. 'I had to finish my report' he always argued in response to her complaints. He never saw the kids anymore. It was weeks since he'd taken Tom to a soccer match, too intent on preparation for meetings, shifting paperwork - or something with her. Time for his kids had been buried in a filofax full of dates. Spurs were playing at Old Trafford next week. They were going. Distance was no object, he had alienated his son and needed him back. As for Karen she would get to hear the bedtime stories she had always asked him for. Her daddy was coming home to kiss her goodnight. Her dreams would begin, as his faded into the darkness.

He managed to ease himself from his cosy spot and he walked into the small room at the back of his office, to take a final look. This was where they had spent hours, all their working hours. Just the two of them, oblivious to anything else. The telephone could ring and he would not answer. He had his own affairs to attend to. She always kept him occupied. The larger room was just for show; they never worked together there. He turned the corner and there she was. Beautiful and perfect, just sitting on the desk. Silent as the commuters on the train. She had been there the entire time waiting to entice him into further projects, but tonight she could not persuade him to stay late, it was over.

He touched her face, hot having worked hard all day, blank she had switched off uncaring. He mumbled 'Goodbye', there was no more to say. Tomorrow another man would prize her. He put his resignation on the desk, turned off the light and finally covered her keyboard.

To Catch the Wind

by

Jeni Waterfield

The wind, blowing straight in from the sea, carried layers of scents that shuffled in the air and teased Peggy's nostrils. She raised her face and sniffed appreciatively. Rotting seaweed, salt, spume. The occasional sharp tang of cliff-top flowers overlaid with the heady, clean taste of ozone. The sweet cocktail drove her wild with the need to fling out her arms and throw back her head in ecstasy, just as she had done as a small girl.

Whatever happened to the town, that cancerous growth of hideous brick and metal whose strung lights marched ever further into the countryside, some things could never be reduced: the sea, the mighty cliffs, that all-pervading wind, sometimes gentle, sometimes wild.

As a child, she had loved to run, her feet delighting in the spongy turf that capped the cliff-top, running, always running, arms spread wide as though to catch the wind. She had left behind her troubled childhood; her whole life that seemed to worsen the older she became. She had run until she was too old to run anymore. Now, far too often, Peggy forgot her joy in the elements and allowed the grey modernisation, spreading its poisonous tentacles about her, to weigh her spirits down. Her shoulders would sag, her head bow, but then once more the wind would blow and, in an instant, all would be forgotten in the wildness, the exhilaration that swept her before it.

Peggy picked up her carrier bags, excitement lending fluidity to her lumpy hands and swollen feet. She began to make her way down the steep main street towards the sea, at once aware that this was no ordinary wind. While she had nodded in her doorway, dreaming, it had built steadily and now it was no easy matter to struggle against it. But it drew her, none-the-less, as it always had. It seemed to be playing with her. Sometimes it punched up the street like a fist, stopping the breath in her chest. At other times, it took her by surprise, sweeping at her from side alleys with a gusty laugh that made her stagger off the pavement.

Despite the effort it took just to keep going, Peggy was aware of other rags of humanity blowing about her. There, in the glow of the street lamp, a young couple clung, the girl's skirt bellied up behind her like a sail. A crowd of drunks lurched from a pub doorway, spilling light and noise onto the pavement. Meeting the blast of the wind, they embraced each other and stumbled, loose-limbed up the road, weaving and swaying, their shouts and songs gusting crazily away like dry leaves. Apart from these few encounters, Peggy saw no-one, though the street seemed peopled by the eddies of dust and litter, spinning in phantom shapes around her.

Still the wind grew. She walked in a funnel of sound, plodding into the throat of the storm. She no longer knew what she was doing here, why she had left her usual nightly sanctuary. But she felt an urge to reach the sea, to escape from the lee of the buildings into the belly of the storm.

The full force of the wind hit her as she turned the corner at the end of the street, throwing her off balance so that she sat down heavily, dropping her bags with the shock. She watched helplessly as they burst open, scattering her few possessions across the pavement before wheeling away ghost-like over the roof-tops above her.

Pulling herself up, she fought her way across the street towards the sound of breakers that crashed against the sea wall, adding their voices to that of the wind in a triumphant hymn to chaos. Reaching the sea wall, she gripped the iron rail and leaned over, gasping at the view that opened out before her.

Careering clouds tossed in tattered pennants as the sea raced towards the wall. Huge white horses gathered, foaming and bellowing, rearing up before hurling themselves against the stonework. Within seconds, Peggy was drenched.

Lifting her face to the spray, she leant into the wall, into the wind, and flung out her arms, surrendering to sensation. She looked up and felt her heart racing with the speeding sky. Through eyes narrowed against the stinging salt, she gazed over the tumbling waters and something inside her, something that had been long asleep, awoke. She shrieked to the wind - with the wind - her voice like a small bird thrown into the air and carried along in exultation.

Peggy did not know how long she stayed there, joining her voice to that of the storm. At last she felt drained, at peace, as if all her sorrows, all her cares, had shifted onto that boiling sea and into the heart of the wind. They were gone like specks of sand and, with their departure, she, too, turned to leave. The wind nudged her from behind now. It bore her easily onto the grand white steps of the hotel opposite and leant her against a pillar.

There, she sank gratefully down and turned her face once more into the wind. Did she imagine it or was its fury abating? It no longer bruised her flesh or seared her eyes but stirred in her hair and caressed her cheek.

She nestled against the shoulder of the wind, that touched her, now, like the lover she had never had, kissing her throat, her hair, her eyes. Then, with a new gentleness, it drew from her lips the last, slow murmur of her breath.

A Coat of many Colours

by

Simon Taylor

I can still remember the day we first met him. I remember it well, for it was my tenth birthday. We did not know what his real name was; so we called him Joseph, because he wore a coat of many colours. We would laugh at the way he was dressed, but he didn't seem to mind, he said his coat had been in his family for generations.

It was so hot that day; it must have been the height of summer. The three of us were playing football in the park; when all at once the sky turned as black as night. It seemed to last for no more than a second. It was at that moment that he appeared.

Jason seemed to take an instant dislike to Joseph. He picked up the ball and marched towards him. His eyes were ablaze, and every muscle in his body seemed flexed. His pug ugly face screwed up into a scowl, and he spat his words out through broken teeth.

'What you staring at?'

Joseph's sad blue eyes were like silhouettes as they stared out through his long brown hair. He looked so small and weak, but his eyes seemed so wise. It seemed like an eternity before he spoke, and then he finally said, 'Can I play too?'

'Just get lost.' Jason snarled.

Tony and I watched as Joseph walked away. We both felt kind of sorry for him.

'We could let him play.' We said in unison.

Jason seemed to feel threatened by Joseph's presence, but reluctantly he agreed to let him play. We kicked the ball around the park for half an hour until finally Jason became tired of the game. His dark eyes stared into Joseph's, and then suddenly he grabbed him by the throat almost lifting him off the ground. His voice was as sharp as a razor; almost cutting through every syllable.

'If you want to join our gang you'll have to prove yourself.'

Jason finally released his grip on Joseph. He stood there laughing as Joseph collapsed to the ground, but Jason wasn't finished yet. He grabbed hold of Joseph by his long brown hair, and dragged him through the woods, and down to the old railway bridge.

We stood there and watched as he pushed Joseph down the grass bank. There was a loud splash as he fell in the water and mud below. He was no more than a few feet from the track. Jason just stood there laughing and leaned against the fence. He watched in delight as Joseph crawled out of the mud below.

It was then as Jason's laughter grew louder that the fence gave way. We watched in horror as he fell to an almost certain death. His body lay there dazed on the track. He was just inches from the live rail. The 5.15 to London roared it's way towards him.

It took Joseph no more than a split second to pull him clear, but Jason began to panic. Joseph lost his balance. His arm was badly burned as he fell on the track. He just had time to free himself as the speeding train flew past.

Jason and Joseph made their way up the bank towards us. Joseph's arm was bleeding badly, and he was covered in mud. Jason was limping slightly otherwise he seemed unharmed. We waited for Jason to speak, but he never even thanked Joseph. He just limped his way up the road. We felt contempt for him from that day on.

Joseph just smiled at us. 'See you tomorrow,' he said.

We went to the park the very next day. We sat there and watched as the sky turned as black as night. Then Joseph would appear in his coat of many colours. We thought that Jason would be the best of friends with him now, but we were wrong. He seemed to resent him even more.

Joseph smiled at Jason. It was a smile that offered friendship, but Jason did not respond in the same manner. Instead he raised his fist, and punched Joseph in the face. The blood ran slowly down Joseph's nose. 'That's for trying to kill me yesterday.'

'But he saved your life,' sniffed Tony nervously.

'Just shut up, and blow your nose; unless you want the same,' said Jason angrily.

Joseph wiped the blood from his face. He took some sandwiches from his pocket, and offered them round. There was only three; so Joseph went without. As we sat there on the grass eating Joseph watched us. I felt moved by him even then. We had treated him so badly; yet he was still willing to let us share his food. It was as if he would rather starve than see us go without.

We met him in the park at the same time everyday. He would tell us stories. We sat there, and listened as he took us to another world. Even Jason would listen in silence. It was then that we realized that we really loved Joseph. He was the best friend we ever had, but we never told him.

It was on the last day of summer that tragedy struck. We were running across the main road, and Joseph got left behind. I remember Jason called him a coward. We watched as Joseph ran straight in front of a car, he didn't stand a chance. The car didn't even stop.

We felt so guilty now. We stared at Joseph's lifeless body as it lay there in the gutter. He was all battered, and covered in blood. There was still a smile on his face. He seemed so at peace now, so silent in his coat of many colours.

There was an old lady who came out of a house nearby. She said she had called an ambulance. She asked us if we knew Joseph. All three of us shook our heads; we denied we had ever known him. We watched as the white ambulance took Joseph away. We felt so ashamed.

The next day we still went to the park, but we just sat there in silence. We did this for three days. it was on the third day we tried to carry on. We took our football to the park, and pretended nothing had even happened. We hadn't seen the sun for days now. As we played the sky went as black as night. Then we heard a voice say - 'Can I play too?'

We stared in awe at Joseph in his coat of many colours. He was still smiling; that smile we knew so well. He looked just like he had looked on that day we had first met him. He stayed with us all day. We shared his food, and he told us stories, and after that day we never saw him again.

The seasons have come and gone, and we've grown old. We take our children to the park now. We watch them as they play, and sometimes as the sky goes as black as night; I can almost see a little boy with long brown hair, still dressed in his coat of many colours.

Ethel's 'Opping

by

Nora Veysey

Ethel sat on the seat on the village green, seeing nothing of what went on around her. The village hadn't really changed - had it? The pub had a new coat of paint and a new sign but then it had probably had several in the years since she'd last seen it. The shop was gone - at least the building was still there but it was a private house now. There were curtains over the large windows that she remembered filled with packets of this and that in pyramids and patterns - oh how she remembered!

The village seemed very quiet. Back in the thirties she had always seen it filled with hop-pickers like herself - spilling out of the pub and the shops, noisy, quarrelsome and completely at variance with the locals.

Every year she came with her parents, her sisters, her brother, her grandparents and various aunts, uncles and cousins. They left their home in Walworth carrying assorted bags, cases, boxes and anything else that would hold the goods and clothes that they needed for 'oppin'. She had gazed out of the windows of the slowly moving train and at every station she had asked 'Is this 'oppin' Mum?'

'Not yet lass - long way yet.' Was the regular answer.

When the family left the train there was a race for the lorries. Every year old Charlie was there, recognising them all and commenting on how much the children had grown.

'Won't be able to sit you in the bin this year, will they young Ethel!'

He never seemed to get any older - but then he had always been old. Ethel thought he must have been born driving a lorry.

It didn't take long to reach the farm and the children cheered as they turned in at the gate. Past the cottages they went, past the stables, past the office, past the wagon lodge and on to the hop-huts. There was chaos until everyone was settled into their own huts, trying desperately, and in the main unsuccessfully, to make the place look a bit more homelike. There's not much you can do to a ten-foot square wooden shed with bare earth for a floor and a bedspring taking up almost half of it.

But all the discomfort was forgotten in the hop-garden. Ethel loved the hops - the cool green tunnels before the bins moved in, the smell of them, even the scratchy feel of them. She was happy to help her mum pick them - earning the money for her winter clothes, but most of all she loved the times when she could run and play with the other children. Sometimes they rode on the top of the cart as it took the hops back to the oast-house, then they could ferret around in the farmyard till the cart did its return journey.

Once every year they were allowed to look into the oast and see the huge fires that dried the hops. The hop-driers lived in the oast right through 'oppin' and their wives or children brought them their meals. Drapes of sacking hid their beds from prying eyes - and draughts. Above the fires were the great piles of hops - dried, drying and waiting to be dried. The thing that fascinated Ethel most was the hole in the floor where the hop-pocket was fastened. The dried hops were tipped into it and pressed down with a heavy weight. You could break your knuckles if you tried to punch the hop-pocket. It was as hard as rock.

Oh the freedom of it all! Lanes to wander, woods to explore, fields to play in, a stream to dam and paddle in, nuts and blackberries to gather, birds and animals to watch - rabbits racing across the fields in the early morning or as the dusk began to close in - little things that scurried away as you approached them - all so different from Walworth.

Ethel had always intended to come back, but so many things got in the way. She never married. Her soldier sweetheart was killed at Arnhem and she didn't fancy anyone else, but as a spinster aunt she was always in demand.

'When I retire,' she said to herself 'that's when I'll go back.' Not to Walworth, she never wanted to see Walworth again, but to 'oppin'. 'Opping' was Nostalgia with a capital N Childhood with a capital C. But she had been ill after her retirement and had needed an operation which had left her weak for a long time and not able to make the necessary effort.

There had been no lorry to meet her at the station today, but taxis were readily available and she soon found herself following the long-ago road to the farm. She had asked the driver to come back for her at four o'clock. She wanted to walk through the farm and savour every inch. She was sure that no one would mind if she explained. Deep down inside was the merest germ of a hope that one of those little cottages might be empty and available to rent - she might even just manage to buy one if she planned very carefully. They were very small she knew, but that was all that she needed. She would love to end her days here.

The bus pulled up by the green and then moved on. No-one boarded it, no-one got off. Ethel had taken no notice of the cars as they went by - buses were almost empty now. Her eyes misted over again.

The cluster of cottages by the farm gate were now one very desirable country property with a large garden and a double garage. As she entered the farm she looked towards the stables and the wagon lodge - two more very up-market homes - the barn, the oast, a very expensive enclave. Even the farmyard was gone, taken up by the gardens of the grand houses.

Shock held her quite still, her dreams disappearing one by one. A lady came out of the stable block.

'Excuse me, you look a trifle lost. Can I help you?' She sounded kind.

'It's just - I used to come here 'oppin' back in the thirties. I wanted to see the 'ops again and the oast and....' Her voice trailed off.

'Oh dear, we don't have hops anymore, just fruit for the P.Y.O. market.'

'P.Y.O.'

'You know, Pick Your Own - apples, raspberries, strawberries, blackcurrants....'

'No 'ops at all?'

'Not anymore. I say are you alright?'

Pride straightened Ethel's back and held her eyes steady. 'Oh yes, quite alright thank you. I'll be going now - I've got a train to catch,' and as an afterthought 'you've been most helpful.'

So now she sat on the seat on the village green. Two more hours to wait until the taxi came and nothing to do. She looked across the road and saw the sign that said 'Teas'.

'That used to be a butcher's shop.' She thought 'Oh well, why not!'

It was quite pleasant inside the tea-shop, panelling and furniture of dark wood, and plants, home-made jams and chocolates for sale. There were no other customers and the lady who brought her tea was more than ready to chat.

'Oh yes, it's quiet at the moment, but we've two coach loads booked in this afternoon - you know - Senior Citizens mystery tour. We get quite a lot of that sort of thing - and it's surprising how many people come to see the church and the old Tudor buildings. Of course in the spring there's the Blossom Route and in the summer it's fruit pickers and in the autumn it's the hop garden tours. We keep busy. You're a stranger here aren't you?'

'I am now. I used to come 'oppin' fifty odd years ago. I wanted to see the old place again.'

'You'll have noticed some differences I'll be bound. Nothing stands still. And that reminds me, I'd better get on. I could do with another pair of hands, I can tell you. I can only get help now and again, nothing really regular. Do you know, there's a little flat over the shop I never use at all. I live in the bungalow behind, but no-one's interested. Every-one here can get as much work as they want in the town and earn far more than I can afford to pay. Oh well, dear, enjoy your tea. You can wait there for as long as you like.'

She bustled off to the kitchen leaving a deep calm behind her - and the growing excitement of a wonderful idea.

Ethel put down her cup very firmly. She straightened her shoulders and lifted her head. She glanced at her watch - three o'clock. The taxi would be back in an hour and there was a lot of sorting out to do before then.

Very deliberately she picked up her cup and saucer and walked towards the kitchen.